A HEROINE CALLED RAHAB

THE CALLED
BOOK 8

KENNETH A. WINTER

WildernessLessons

JOIN MY READERS' GROUP FOR UPDATES AND FUTURE RELEASES

Please join my Readers' Group so i can send you a free book, as well as updates and information about future releases, etc.

See the back of the book for details on how to sign up.

A Heroine Called Rahab

"The Called" – Book 8 (a series of novellas)

Published by:

Kenneth A. Winter

WildernessLessons, LLC

Richmond, Virginia

United States of America

kenwinter.org

wildernesslessons.com

Edited by Sheryl Martin Hash

Cover design by Scott Campbell Design

ISBN 978-1-9568661-4-8 (soft cover)

ISBN 978-1-9568661-5-5 (e-book)

ISBN 978-1-9568661-6-2 (large print)

Library of Congress Control Number: 2022922381

The basis for the story line of this book is taken from the Book of Joshua. Certain fictional events or depictions of those events have been added.

DEDICATION

To the heroines in my life
who overcame overwhelming hurdles and walked by faith

∽

It was by faith . . .
(Hebrews 11:31)

∽

CONTENTS

FROM THE AUTHOR

A word of explanation for those of you who are new to my writing.

You will notice that whenever i use the pronoun "I" referring to myself, i have chosen to use a lowercase "i." This only applies to me personally (in the Preface). i do not impose my personal conviction on any of the characters in this book. It is not a typographical error. i know this is contrary to proper English grammar and accepted editorial style guides. i drive editors (and "spell check") crazy by doing this. But years ago, the Lord convicted me – personally – that in all things i must decrease and He must increase.

And as a way of continuing personal reminder, from that day forward, i have chosen to use a lowercase "i" whenever referring to myself. Because of the same conviction, i use a capital letter for any pronoun referring to God throughout the entire book. The style guide for the New Living Translation (NLT) does not share that conviction. However, you will see that i have intentionally made that slight revision and capitalized any pronoun referring to God in my quotations of Scripture from the NLT. If i have violated any style guides as a result, please accept my apology, but i must honor this conviction.

Lastly, regarding this matter – this is a <u>personal</u> conviction – and i share it only so you will understand why i have chosen to deviate from normal editorial practice. i am in no way suggesting or endeavoring to have anyone else subscribe to my conviction. Thanks for your understanding.

PREFACE

~

This fictional novella is the eighth book in the series titled, *The Called*. Like the others, it is a story about an ordinary person God called to use in extraordinary ways. As i've said in my previous books, we tend to elevate the people we read about in Scripture and place them on a pedestal far beyond our reach because of the faith they exhibited. We tend to think, "Of course God used them. They had extraordinary strength or extraordinary faith. But God could never use an ordinary person like me."

But nothing could be further from the truth. The reality is that throughout history, God has used the ordinary to accomplish the extraordinary – and He has empowered them through His Holy Spirit – just as He still does today!

Rahab was one of those people. Yes, the Bible tells us she was a prostitute. That means she was a sinner, just like you and me. Our sins may look different . . . but at the end of the day, we are all sinners. Yes, she was separated from God – because that's what sin does – it separates us from a Holy God. But because of His mercy and His grace, He chose to make a way to redeem us from our sin – just like He did Rahab.

We are told very little about her in Scripture, except perhaps the most important thing! She is listed in the "Hall of Fame" as recorded in the Book of Hebrews:

It was by faith that Rahab the prostitute did not die with all the others in her city who refused to obey God. For she had given a friendly welcome to the spies.[1]

In this story, i attempt to paint a picture of what life may have been like for Rahab growing up in Jericho and leading up to the day she met the Israelite spies. i imagine she had a hard life with many difficulties and heartbreaks to overcome. But i also believe she was a woman of courage and strength. Even though Rahab didn't acknowledge her Creator during the earlier years of her life, He gave her the courage and strength to take a bold stand by faith. i believe there is much we can learn from her. So, i hope you'll enter into this story with an open mind and allow Rahab to challenge you in your personal walk with God.

As you are already aware, i titled this book *A Heroine Called Rahab* – **not** *A Prostitute Called Rahab*. i did so as a reminder that God sees us for who we are as we walk with Him by faith; He doesn't see us through the lens of the sin from which He has redeemed us. i for one am so grateful that He doesn't look at me as "a liar called Ken" or "a cheater called Ken"; rather, He looks at me as well as you through the lens of His precious Son – our Lord and Savior, Jesus Christ.

The basic story comes from the Book of Joshua, specifically chapters two through six. I have endeavored to create a historical background for the Canaanite city of Jericho, though much has been lost in the annals of history. Even though the Canaanites were descendants from Noah – just as we all are – their forebearers had long before turned away from the God of Noah and turned to the pagan gods of Baal and Asherah. Most often, the rituals they practiced in the worship of their goddess Asherah involved prostitution. Accordingly, you will find i have chosen to write this story in that light. Instead of a brothel, i refer to a pagan temple. Instead of a prostitute, i refer to a temple priestess. i do so to remind us of the pagan beliefs that ruled Jericho in that day. i also do so as a reminder that it was a very dark place.

It was so dark that God did not want any remnant of the city to survive that could possibly lead His people astray. In our day and time, we often struggle with how a loving God could totally eradicate a people – part of His creation – like He did the Jerichoites. But we lose sight that He gave the Jerichoites and all the other people in those lands ample opportunity to turn to Him. They knew of the God of the Israelites. They knew of His power and His person. They knew He was unlike any god they were worshiping. And yet, they rejected Him and chose to continue in their sinful practices.

As much as God loved them, He is also a just God and He will by no means clear the guilty.[2] The people of Jericho fell under His judgment – except one, together with her family, who trusted Him by faith. But the story of Rahab's faith doesn't stop there. We see the impact she had on the generations that followed. Her son Boaz became the kinsman redeemer of a young Moabite woman by the name of Ruth. Her great-grandson David, a shepherd boy, would become the king of Israel. And through her descendants, the King of kings would one day make His advent into this world!

So, i invite you to sit back and join Rahab as she tells you the story of her life. She will introduce you to a variety of people – some of whom were real people taken from the pages of Scripture, and others who have been fabricated for the purpose of telling this story. You will find i have added fictional background details about some of the real people so we might see them as people and not simply as names.

i have also given names to those we know existed but remained unnamed in the Bible, most notably the rulers of Jericho and Rahab's family members. Included as an appendix in the back of this book is a character listing to clarify the historical vs. fictional elements of each character.

Whenever i directly quote Scripture, it is italicized. The Scripture references are also included as an appendix in the book. The remaining instances of dialogue related to individuals from Scripture that are not italicized are a part of the fictional story that helps advance the narrative.

i hope this book will prompt you to read the biblical account of Rahab's life and how God led His people to inhabit the land He had prepared for them. None of my books is intended to be a substitute for God's Word – rather, i hope they will lead you to spend time in His Word.

Finally, as i have already indicated, my prayer is you will see Rahab through fresh eyes – and be challenged to live out *your* walk with the Lord with the same courage and faith she displayed. And most importantly, i pray you will be challenged to be an "ordinary" follower with the willingness and faith to be used by God in extraordinary ways that will impact not only this generation, but also the generations to come . . . until our Lord returns!

~

1

STRANGERS IN THE CITY

~

"My brother and I need a room for the night," the older and obviously more confident of the two men said as the siblings entered the inn.

"I have not seen you two here before," I replied. "Is it just a room that you require?"

"We'd like food and drink as well," the younger man added.

"Of course! And anything else?" I inquired. "Have you, perhaps, also come to express your worship to the goddess Asherah?"

I knew before I asked the question that these men had no interest in bedding one of my priestesses. It was obvious who they were and where they were from, but I was not going to let them know that I knew – at least just yet.

"No, we have no interest in doing so," the older man answered, evidently the spokesman for the two. The younger man was looking at the floor, apparently somewhat embarrassed by my question.

"Who are you, stranger?" I asked. "And what brings the two of you to Jericho?"

"We are weary travelers from Moab on our way to Hebron," he answered. "We have stopped to rest for the night before we continue our journey in the morning. One of your officials at the city gate directed us to your inn to find lodging accommodations."

I didn't tell them I had seen them earlier when they spoke with Chemosh after he approached them at the gate. Very little happens in Jericho that I don't see or know about. These men had stood out to him, just as conspicuously as they stood out to me. They may think they have us all fooled – but that is not the case. They are no more travelers from Moab than I am. But these Israelites may just be the ones I need to carry out my plan. I will play along with them for now.

"The official failed to mention the priestesses also reside here," the younger man nervously interjected as I nodded.

"And what are your names?" I inquired.

"My name is Iru, and my brother's name is Elah," the older man replied.

I looked Iru straight in the eyes and said, "My name is Rahab. I am the overseer of this inn. Please know that you are most welcome! We will do everything we can to make your stay with us satisfactory and provide you with the best hospitality Jericho has to offer. Go, recline at one of the tables and make yourselves comfortable. One of my attendants will bring you something to eat and drink."

A short time later, as they were finishing their meal, I approached the table. "Gentlemen, I trust the food has been to your liking, and you have eaten your fill." Both men nodded their approval and extended their compliments. Now that their stomachs were full and they were relaxed, I introduced the conversation I truly wanted to have with them.

"In your travels here from Moab, you must have passed through the encampment of the Israelites on the other side of the river. How did they receive you as you walked among them?"

I could tell they hadn't anticipated my question. "Our peoples are distant cousins to one another," Iru replied. "Our ancestor Lot was the nephew of their patriarch Abraham, so they treated us cordially and allowed us to pass through them without restriction."

"That surprises me, because I have heard the Israelites distrust your people," I said. "As a matter of fact, I am told that an Israelite high priest ran a spear through an Israelite man simply because he had brought a Moabite woman into his tent. That doesn't sound very cordial to me."

"You appear to be better informed about what occurs in the Israelite camp than we are," Iru responded with mock surprise. "Gratefully, we did not encounter any such hostility," he added.

"Well, I doubt you would have encountered any – since the two of you really aren't Moabites, are you?" I asked without any animosity.

The men looked warily at me, then glanced around the room to see who else might be listening to our conversation.

"Do not be concerned, gentlemen," I continued. "I mean you no harm. Actually, I believe we can be allies. All of us who live in the land of Canaan are acutely aware of how your God has gone before your people, defeating the Egyptians by drowning them in the sea. And how he defeated King Sihon of the Amorites and King Og of Bashan. We know that not a single survivor remained in those lands after your people came to occupy them.

"Such is the fear in Jericho. We fear your God will destroy us all. It is well-known your God told you He will give you all the land from the Negev Desert in the south to the Lebanon mountains in the north, from the Euphrates River on the east to the Mediterranean Sea on the west. These are the lands of the Canaanites, the Hittites, the Amorites, the Perizzites, the Hivites, and the Jebusites. We do not fear your armies, but we do fear your God! And we know that our city, Jericho, now stands between your people and the rest of the land."

The two Israelites no longer tried to conceal their identity, so I continued.

"The two of you have obviously been sent to spy on our city and its defenses. It was likely just as obvious to Chemosh when you encountered him at the gate. I believe your God has brought us together because I can help you – and in turn, you can help me!"

"Why would you help us?" Iru asked.

"I have my reasons," I replied, "but, at this moment, they are not your concern."

Suddenly there was a loud pounding on the door to the inn, and a voice called out, "Rahab, I have a message for you from our king!"

I looked at the two men and said, "Very soon, I will need to trust you. But for right now, you must trust me. Follow me! Quickly!"

2

IT ALL STARTED WITH A CURSE

~

*B*efore I tell you more about what happened that night, I need to give you some background. This story actually began 900 years ago.

The ancients living in our city speak of a great flood that covered the earth. All living things on the land and of the air perished in those waters. That is, except for a man named Noah and his family. They, along with a male and female of every bird and animal, survived the flood inside a large ark constructed for that purpose. The ancients attribute the survival of everyone in that ark to our gods, Baal and Asherah. But I now know the flood was, in fact, a judgment sent by the God of the Israelites – the One who had originally created all life – in order to cleanse the earth of unrighteousness. And Noah was deemed by Jehovah God to be the only blameless man through whom humankind would again multiply and populate the earth.

One year after the rains had begun, the floodwaters receded and Noah, his wife, their sons and daughters-in-law left the ark along with all the animals and birds. Noah's sons – Shem, Ham, and Japheth – joined him as they immediately set out cultivating the land.

The ancients say that one night, a few years after returning to dry land, Noah unintentionally became drunk on the wine he had made from the harvest of his vineyard. He lay naked in a drunken stupor on the ground in his tent. His middle son, Ham, walked into the tent and discovered his father. But instead of covering him, Ham went outside and spoke disrespectfully about his father to his brothers. When they heard of their father's condition, Shem and Japheth walked backward into the tent, so as not to see their father's nakedness, and covered his body with a blanket.

The next day, when Noah awoke and learned what Ham had done, he cursed the descendants of Ham through Ham's eldest son, Canaan, saying:

> *"A curse on the Canaanites!*
> *May they be the lowest of servants*
> *to the descendants of Shem and Japheth."*[1]

I, together with everyone living in this region, can follow our ancestry back to Canaan. Some would say we are the victims of that curse. Others say we have had to work harder and fight with a vengeance to overcome the difficulties of that curse. As the account has been passed down through the generations, there is no question it has made us a belligerent people, warring against anyone who threatens to exercise dominion over us.

I am part of the seventeenth generation from Ham, and I can assure you the distrust and conviction nurtured by the knowledge of that curse courses through my veins. And in my case, my distrust runs deeply after generations of abuse brought on by people who simply thought they could.

You also need to know that the Israelites are descended from Shem. Their patriarch, Abraham, is the ninth generation from Shem. As we watch their number assembling nearby on the other side of the Jordan River, the prophetic nature of what Noah said – that we will be servants to the descendants of Shem – is not lost on those of us familiar with the curse.

∽

Our city was first established as a small farming village six generations before me. Most of the first inhabitants were farmers who had come to this region seeking a plot of land where they could prosper. This region, in the midst of what has been called "the fertile crescent," is considered by many to be the most fruitful. We are surrounded by numerous natural springs, which help produce rich vegetation in a very moderate climate. As a result, the farmers found what they were seeking, and as the years passed, more people followed.

The village soon grew into a town, and after three generations became an important city. Its prosperity not only attracted other farmers seeking success and fortune, but it also began to attract other tribes and nations that sought to take the land from our people.

Most notable among them were the Egyptians. Their king, Ahmose I, as well as his son, Amenhotep, led their armies to assert control over an expanding region that reached well into our part of the world. Jericho's burgeoning success made the city a ripe prize for the taking, and the city lacked any natural defenses to protect it.

A man named Shachar, together with his older brother, Hadad, recognized the increasing vulnerability of our city. They challenged the leaders to begin construction of a defensive wall surrounding Jericho. Since the majority of our city's residents were farmers, very few had any military experience or knowledge of how to build a defensive structure that would repel an enemy's attack.

Though Shachar and Hadad also lacked that experience, they possessed an innate ability to design, plan, and lay the foundations of a wall that would ultimately take over 100 years to complete.

The wall surrounding Jericho is actually three walls. First, the mound, or "tell," upon which the wall is built, is surrounded by a great earthen embankment with a stone retaining wall at its base. That wall is fifteen feet high. On top of the retaining wall is a mudbrick wall measuring six feet thick and twenty-five feet high.

Then from the crest of the embankment is a similar mudbrick wall that is also six feet thick and starts at forty-six feet above ground level (outside the retaining wall), rising an additional twenty-five feet into the air. From the ground level these walls project seventy feet into the air. Shachar and Hadad, as well as those who followed them in the work, took great care and pride in building what they thought was an impregnable fortress.

No descendant of Shem or Japheth would ever become master over the people of Jericho . . . or so they thought!

3

TWO COUSINS

◇

*T*wenty years after construction of the wall commenced, the need for it took on even greater importance. Many years earlier, a people of mixed Canaanite and Asian descent, who called themselves the Hyksos, had invaded Egypt. They controlled a large portion of that nation for slightly more than 100 years until they were driven out by Egypt's King Ahmose.

The Hyksos leaders retreated from Egypt and took up residence in and around the Canaanite city of Lachish in the Negev Desert. However, Ahmose was not content to merely drive the Hyksos out of Egypt. He dispatched his army to Canaan to completely destroy the Hyksos. And destroy them, he did, taking control of the city within a matter of days. Ahmose's commander immediately declared the city to be a part of the kingdom of Egypt.

Shockwaves rippled throughout Canaan. Did Ahmose have his eye on all our cities? Would we all be conquered by Egypt? Efforts on building our defensive walls were doubled. Additionally, the leaders of Jericho saw the need to take two further actions.

Up until then, Jericho had been governed by a council selected by the residents. But as Jericho grew in size and stature, the council saw the need to select a king – one who would lead the city to achieve greater strength and prosperity, and one who would lead us to be better prepared to stave off invading forces. Only two men rose to the top of the list to be considered for that position. They were Attar, son of Hadad; and Kirta, son of Shachar.

The two cousins were already leading the work in constructing the wall, having taken over the responsibility from their fathers. They set plans in motion to accelerate the work. But beyond that, the two men had very different views of what the king's role should be. Attar saw the kingship as an opportunity to advance his own personal station and lord his will over the people. Kirta, on the other hand, believed the king should be a servant leader of the people, shepherding the city to greater achievements for the betterment of all its citizens.

Attar, however, was the more masterful communicator, and that enabled him to convince the council he was the preferable choice. One of his promises was to nurture an alliance with the other Canaanite cities, which would provide a more unified fighting force in the event Egypt, or any other nation, threatened attack. Though Attar and Kirta agreed that the creation of such an alliance was important, Attar's primary motivation was the increased power and position he would achieve as the leader of such an alliance.

Kirta was acutely aware of Attar's ambitions and took every opportunity to keep his cousin's more selfish motives in check. As you can imagine, King Attar became incensed by what he described as Kirta's flagrant disloyalty. Their conflict rose to its pinnacle when Attar proposed to double the taxes being collected from residents. The current portion was being used to fund the construction of the wall. Attar announced that the increased taxes would be used to build a palace and provide an income for the king. Kirta was the first to speak up in opposition.

Again, however, Attar masterfully explained to the people that he was simply trying to enable Jericho to maintain its standing among the other great cities of Canaan. After all, if Jericho was going to be one of the leading cities of Canaan, it needed to have a palace that reflected the city's importance and stature. "I do not seek a palace for myself; rather, I seek only its benefit to the city!" Attar declared.

As for the objections over an income, Attar added, "Those funds will merely enable me to conduct the affairs that you have charged me to undertake as your king."

The council subserviently acquiesced to his proposal. It soon became clear that the men, whose role had originally been to keep their new king in check, had simply become his footmen, catering to his every whim and demand.

As time passed, Attar's self-serving actions became more brazen, and Kirta became even more adamant in his objections. The king did not tolerate such criticism for long and eventually decided to eliminate his voice of opposition.

Attar fabricated a story that Kirta was secretly colluding with the Egyptians to undermine the city for his own personal gain. Attar had reigned as king for five years when he had Kirta arrested and brought before him.

"Kirta, you are charged with committing acts of treason against your city, your fellow neighbors, and your king!" Attar declared. "You have clandestinely engaged in traitorous liaisons with the Egyptians in order to undermine our alliances with neighboring tribes and cities, and weaken our ability to defend ourselves against an attack. You have sought to do harm to your king and your neighbors. In so doing, you have also defamed the reputation of one of the great men of our city – your father – my Uncle Shachar."

"What proof do you have of these charges?" Kirta asked.

"The testimonies of six members of our distinguished council!" Attar responded.

One after another the council members stepped forward and brought false accusations against Kirta. Their testimonies were so outlandish that they placed him in three different cities at the exact same time. But no one questioned the councilmen or called attention to their obvious error. They had said exactly what they had been instructed to say, and no one would dare contradict them – or more importantly, the king.

When the false witnesses had finished bringing their charges, the king rose from his seat and declared, "I cannot listen to any more of this! Kirta, you are to be taken out of the city and beheaded for your treason immediately! May all of Jericho know what you have done, and may all of our enemies know that we will take swift action against anyone who threatens us in this way. May the shame of your actions continue to be borne by your family!"

∼

4

ENSLAVED!

~

*K*irta's five-year-old son, Llisha, was forced to stand by his mother's side as the two of them witnessed his father's execution that day. As you would expect, the horror left an indelible imprint. The king seized Kirta's home and forced his widow and child to live in the streets as beggars. Llisha's mother soon became overcome by a madness from which she never recovered. After two years of suffering, she was laid in her grave, leaving seven-year-old Llisha to fend for himself.

The only memories the lad could recall of his young life were the terror of his father's death and the agony of his mother's insanity. Additionally, King Attar made sure Llisha was forever branded as a traitor's son. After his mother died, Llisha was sentenced by the king to work as a slave on the city wall. No one seemed to remember that Llisha's grandfather was one of the original designers of the wall or that his father had once been considered for the position of king. In the eyes of the people of Jericho, there was no one of a lower station than young Llisha.

Soon after Llisha's father was executed, King Ahmose of Egypt died. His son, Amenhotep, the new pharaoh of Egypt, determined that with the eradication of the Hyksos leaders there was no benefit for continued attacks on the other Canaanite cities. Pharaoh's army returned to Egypt, and Jericho, as well as the other Canaanite cities, were no longer under imminent threat of attack. As time passed, the fear of attack became a distant memory and was soon forgotten altogether.

But that's not all the people had forgotten. There was also no longer any memory of the God of Noah, nor the fact that our people had been birthed from the seed of the remnant saved by Jehovah God from the flood. There were stories told of a great flood, but those tales all centered around the vengeance of the god Baal, and our existence was attributed to the kindness of Baal's consort, the goddess Asherah. Accordingly, our people had turned to her and now worshiped her above all other gods.

Under Attar's reign, Jericho soon became a place where good was evil and evil was good. And no one seemed to realize it – or if they did, no one seemed to care.

Llisha's memories of his home and family life from the days before his father's arrest also quickly faded. They had lived happily among the elite of the city, surrounded by finery. But instantly, all of that had been taken away. He and his mother had been forced to live on the streets as beggars until the day the soldiers arrested him and placed him in the charge of the slave masters.

The only good that came from being enslaved was that he was now provided two meals each day – albeit a meager fare – and a place to sleep with a roof over his head. All of the men and boys labored from dawn to dusk on building the city's wall. Most of the women and girls gathered straw and clay to make bricks, some prepared the food for all of the slaves, and some of the younger women and older girls were taken to the temple of Asherah.

A few days after he arrived at the slave quarters, Llisha was befriended by a young husband and wife. They had been slaves since birth and had grown up in that place. They knew firsthand just how frightening slavery was for a child. The slave masters tried to discourage them from having anything to do with the boy. "He is the son of a traitor," they said. "You do not want to associate with him, or the king might decide you are traitors as well!"

But the young couple, my great-grandparents, whose names were Kusor and Pidraya, bravely chose to ignore the warning, saying, "His father may or may not have been a traitor, but that doesn't make this boy one! And we won't treat him like one, unless he gives us cause. So leave us – and him – alone!"

Surprisingly the slave masters did not punish them for their insolence. Instead they just laughed and walked away.

Llisha was shocked. No one had stood up for him since his father was killed! Kusor and Pidraya took it upon themselves to watch over him from that day forward, and he became a member of their family. Their kindness prevented him from being further abused or taken advantage of, and their love and trust enabled hope to return to his life.

Not long after, Pidraya gave birth to a baby girl named Ashima. Llisha became Ashima's big brother and protector from her very first day. And once she was old enough to walk, she was his shadow and constant companion. Pidraya's work assignment was to prepare meals for the slaves. Each day, Llisha and Kusor would go off to work on the wall, and Ashima would help her mother with the meals. And so it continued every day for fifteen years.

As Llisha got older, he learned that women taken to the temple worked as priestesses – or sacred prostitutes. Men entering the temple would pay an offering to the chief priestess to engage in sexual rituals with one of the women or girls in one of the temple's twelve small rooms. The poor were not permitted in the temple since they could not pay the offering. This meant the practice was limited to the wealthy and powerful men of the city. But Llisha never gave the practice much thought. He knew some of the women and girls who were taken there, but he did not know any of them well.

When Llisha was a young man in his mid-twenties, he heard that King Attar had died. Though the city formally mourned his passing, the only emotion Llisha felt was elation. The man who had falsely accused his father and destroyed both of his parents was now dead. Llisha knew that Attar had never paid any price for his crimes in this life, but he prayed to the god Resheph, the lord of the nether world, that Attar would now be tormented forever in death.

As expected, Attar's son, Arsu, became the new king of Jericho. Though Llisha was convinced Arsu was no better than his father, he doubted the son could be any worse. Only time would prove whether or not that belief was accurate. But neither of these events would change the circumstances of his life – or so he thought.

However, a few nights later, an event occurred that would dramatically alter his life. One of the slave masters came to the place where Llisha and his family were having dinner and announced, "Ashima, tomorrow we will take you to the temple to begin your work there as a priestess. Be sure to look your finest when we come for you!"

Suddenly what took place at the temple had become of great concern to Llisha!

～

5

IMPRISONED

～

"We must stop this!" Llisha declared to Kusor and Pidraya.

"We are slaves!" Kusor replied. "There is nothing we can do. If we make any attempt to interfere, we will only cause Ashima more harm, and we will all pay a great price. This is as the gods have ordained. You must accept it, Llisha!"

"But I love Ashima!" Llisha openly announced for the first time. "She is to become my wife!"

"Llisha, that is not your choice," Pidraya said gently. "She has been selected to serve Asherah. It is a great honor for her. Would you prefer that she work here in the kitchens like I do? Or on the wall like you? The gods have given her beauty so she might escape our fate. But do not be mistaken – she is and will always be a slave, without the ability to choose for herself. And neither can we."

"Then I will take her away from Jericho!" Llisha declared.

"You will make no such attempt!" Kusor said angrily. "Such an attempt will end in her death – and yours. Come to your senses, boy! There is nothing you can do!"

Ashima, who had quietly listened to all of this, turned to Llisha and said, "You know my heart belongs to you. I have loved you all my life, and nothing will ever cause that to change. But you must accept this, Llisha. Promise me you will not do anything foolish!"

Llisha replied that he would not – but none of them believed him.

The next morning, the guards delivered Ashima to the chief priestess at the temple. She was immediately taken by the female attendants to be properly bathed and prepared. Only the most powerful men of the city were given the opportunity to lie down with a virgin priestess. The offering price was an unequaled amount that could only be afforded by the wealthiest. And in Ashima's case, her beauty caused the amount to be even greater. Great care was given by the attendants to prepare her.

When she was ready, she was brought to Shahar, the high counselor to the king. In that role, he was second only to the king in importance and power in the city. The chief priestess had told Ashima that it would be a rare honor for her. "If you are pleasing to this man, your time here in the temple will be one of privilege."

Shahar was much older than Ashima's father, and there was no mistaking that he was a man who was used to getting whatever he wanted. He and Ashima occupied the finest of the rooms in the temple for the entire day and well into the night.

Ashima was surprised when he interrupted their time together on two occasions by welcoming one of his subordinates into the room. Though they spoke in hushed tones, Ashima was able to glean that the high counselor was plotting to have King Arsu assassinated. Shahar was even so brash as to say to her before their time had concluded, "Who knows, girl, you may soon find yourself being the priestess to the king!"

At about that same time, Ashima heard a commotion in the open area outside of her room. Throughout the day, the temple had been quiet and serene, but now the silence was broken by the sound of voices shouting at one another. After a few moments, she realized that one of those voices belonged to Llisha. Apparently, he had overtaken the guards at the temple entrance and was now demanding to know where she was.

The door to the room suddenly burst open. For a moment, Llisha just stood in the doorway staring at her and Shahar. His hesitation provided just enough time for a fresh contingent of guards and soldiers to overpower him. They quickly bound him and forced him to the ground.

"Please don't hurt him!" Ashima cried out.

"Who is this man?" Shahar shouted.

"His name is Llisha, and he is like a brother to me," Ashima confessed.

"Well then, in your honor, I will not have Llisha, son of the traitor Kirta, put to death for his insolence," Shahar said. "Instead, I will have him taken to the dungeon where he will live out the rest of his days in chains. Take him away, guards! And Ashima, if you want to continue to enjoy your life of ease here in the temple, you will never make mention of this man again. Otherwise, I will be forced to consider you to be a traitor just like him and have you both executed! Now, return here to me, and perform your duties as a priestess!"

Ashima knew Llisha's fate now rested in her hands. Shahar would have them both killed if she said or did anything that displeased him. So she dried her tears, hid her hatred for Shahar, and did what she had to do.

As the days and weeks passed, Shahar returned to the temple on most days to be with her. Though she did well in disguising her contempt for him, she couldn't look at him without being reminded of Llisha suffering in prison. Shahar became increasingly open in his conversations with his subordinates while she was in the room. He repeatedly told her she would be his priestess when he ruled over the city as king.

The one man who was never expected to come to the temple to worship Asherah was the king. Instead, the priestess he chose always went to his palace. One day, quite unexpectedly, the chief priestess told Ashima that she was being sent to the palace to be with the king.

"The priestess who ordinarily serves the king has become ill, so I am sending you in her place. Make sure you do everything to please the king and gain his favor, just as you have done for his high counselor. If you do, it will bode well for you!"

As the attendants helped my grandmother prepare for her visit with the king, she began to formulate a plan.

❧

6

PRIESTESS TO THE KING

~

*W*hen she arrived at the palace, Ashima was immediately taken to a bed chamber and told to prepare herself for the king's arrival. As the door closed behind her, she was momentarily distracted by the overwhelming size and splendor of the room. She had seen the palace from the outside many times, but she never imagined how grand it was on the inside. Though the rooms at the temple were opulently furnished, they paled in comparison to what she now beheld.

But she only allowed herself a few moments to enjoy her surroundings before turning her attention back to the task at hand. The king was the only person who could possibly help her get Llisha released. If this didn't work, he would either spend the rest of his days in that dungeon or neither of them would have long to live.

My grandmother had just finished her preparations when King Arsu entered the bed chamber through a side door she had failed to notice. "Where is the priestess who normally attends me?" the king asked.

"She has become ill, and the chief priestess wanted to protect the king from becoming infected with her sickness," Ashima replied. "However, the chief priestess wants you to know that the illness is minor, and the girl should be able to return to you in a matter of days. In the meantime, the chief priestess and I pray I will be pleasing to you."

"Well, for all our sakes, I hope you are pleasing to me as well!" he said.

Apparently, the king was not disappointed. To the contrary, he made his pleasure known to Ashima – as well as the chief priestess – and requested my grandmother return to the palace for another visit.

On her second visit to serve the king, Ashima decided it was time to proceed with her plan. "My king, if I have gained any favor in your eyes, would you permit me to tell you something I believe you will want to know?"

The king appeared to be intrigued by her question and instructed her to proceed.

"My king, I have been made aware of a plan to assassinate you," my grandmother began.

"You what?" the king replied. "How would anyone dare do such a thing – and how is it you have knowledge of those plans? Is it another feigned uprising by the slaves? Have you been listening to the riffraff, my dear?"

"No, my king," she countered. "What I am about to tell you, I heard from the lips of your high counselor, Shahar, while he was with me in the temple. He thought I was not paying attention."

She then told King Arsu what Shahar had discussed in front of her. The king interrupted her with questions several times to clarify specific details. Initially, he rejected the idea Shahar could betray him in such a way. But by the time Ashima had finished, the king apparently found credence in her story.

"I want you to remain here while I investigate your story," the king said. "I will place a guard outside the bed chamber – for your protection if you are telling me the truth, and for your detainment should I find you have lied to me!"

Later that day, the king returned to the bed chamber and told my grandmother Shahar would not be carrying out his plan.

"He, and all those who conspired against me with him, have been rounded up and executed," the king declared. "It took courage for you to speak out against the high counselor – even to me. Because of your courage, you saved your king's life. Because of your loyalty, I will now reward you by naming you priestess to the king. No other priestess, other than the chief priestess, will have a higher position in the temple than you. And you alone will serve your king – and you will only serve me here in this bed chamber."

"You honor your servant, my king," my grandmother replied. "But I have only done what any loyal servant should do for her king."

"Yes, but you have done so selflessly – expecting nothing in return," the king said. "And because you have asked for nothing, I will grant you one request. What shall it be? Jewelry? Clothing? Perhaps your own servant?"

Ashima paused for a moment, as if she was pondering his offer, even though she already knew exactly what she would request. "My king, there is one who has been like a brother to me since I was born. Shahar had him imprisoned in the dungeon for merely showing concern for my welfare. If I have pleased the king, I ask you to release him to serve in the temple."

"What is the man's name?" the king asked.

"He is Llisha, son of Kirta," Ashima replied.

The king hesitated and then said, "This man is my cousin and would have enjoyed my great favor if his father had not been a traitor. My father condemned him to a life of slavery because of his father's actions. But you now ask me to show him mercy and release him from the dungeon. I will do so because I agreed to grant you one request, but know that there is a price I will extract from him before I release him to serve in the temple."

Ashima trembled as she asked, "What is that price, my king?"

All the king would say was that the matter would be between Llisha and his king, and that he would be released from the dungeon in one week's time.

The king was true to his word. Llisha was escorted to the temple by the king's guards one week later. When Ashima saw him arrive, she ran to him, threw her arms around him, and greeted him with a kiss.

She exclaimed, "Llisha, my love, the gods and the king have been gracious to us. They have brought you back to me. And now we can be together here in this place without fear and with the blessing of the king."

Llisha soberly pulled himself away from her embrace as he said, "We may have the blessing of the king, but it has not been without its cost. He has told me that you are his priestess – and not mine. In order to leave the dungeon and return to you, I was forced to surrender my manhood. He told me that the only way I could serve near you in the temple was as a eunuch!"

The man who should have been my grandfather … was not to be.

7

CHILDREN OF THE KING

~

*M*y grandmother spent many of her days and nights after that in the bed chamber of the king. She had not expected King Arsu to extract such a price, and she would never forgive him for what he had done to Llisha. But she knew she must bury her hatred deep inside for the sake of them all. She and Llisha always sought to encourage one another whenever they were together; they never again spoke of what had been taken from them.

Five months after Llisha's release from the dungeon, the city heralded the joyous news that King Arsu's queen had given birth to a son, whom the king named Aleyin. He would be the heir to the throne. For a short while, Ashima's trips to the palace became less frequent. But once the queen had become great with child, Ashima was summoned back to the palace.

Three weeks after the birth of the king's son, Ashima awoke one morning in great discomfort. She was grateful she was not scheduled to go to the palace, but she feared the source of her illness. The chief priestess quickly discerned Ashima was with child – the king's child – though no one would ever refer to the baby as such.

The king was alerted, and for the last few months of Ashima's pregnancy, she was excused from making trips to the palace. The chief priestess chose another whom she deemed a suitable substitute. During those months, Llisha was attentive to Ashima's every need. The two of them enjoyed frequent walks outside the city walls – and often momentarily forgot their circumstances.

They were also permitted to visit Ashima's parents, Kusor and Pidraya, whom neither had seen since the day Ashima left to serve in the temple. Though the means by which the baby was conceived grieved them all, the expectant arrival of their first grandchild was a time for rejoicing. A casual observer would have mistaken the visit to be a joyful family reunion of expectant parents and grandparents

When the time came for the baby's birth, Llisha was on hand to assist the chief priestess, who acted as midwife. A few minutes after midnight, a baby's cry shattered the night's silence as Ashima's daughter – my mother – entered this world. She would be named Liluri. Though the city would never herald *her* birth, Ashima and Llisha would always think of her as royalty – if not officially by birth, at least through Llisha's ancestral line. She would not rise above being a servant, nor, more than likely, a priestess – but to them she would always be a princess!

My mother was raised in the temple. When Ashima was away at the palace with the king, Liluri was left in the care of Llisha, her surrogate father. He tended to Liluri as if she were his own daughter – and no one was ever permitted to say anything to the contrary. And to her credit, Ishtar, the chief priestess, kept a protective eye over all of them.

Liluri was not the only child who grew up in the temple. There were other children who were also the products of the priestesses' acts of service. The companionship of other children created a family environ-ment – if not in truth, at least in practice. The children were permitted to remain in the temple until they were eight years old. After that, they were to be turned out as street urchins or slaves. The male leaders who controlled the workings of the temple and the city didn't much care either way.

A boy named Kothar, who was one year older than Liluri, gained the affection of Ishtar early on. He was a handsome lad with strength of character and precocious wisdom. Liluri and he soon became fast friends. Ishtar was determined that neither one would be turned out of the temple on their eighth birthday. She enjoyed a certain amount of influence over the city leaders as a result of the knowledge she had gleaned about them over the years. So no one contested her decision when she declared the two children would become temple servants – Kothar under the supervision of Llisha, and Liluri under her supervision.

As the years passed, the two children blossomed, and their friendship grew. Ishtar made provision for the children to be taught by the same teachers who instructed the king's children. Though the teachers initially protested, they soon found that the chief priestess could be quite persuasive. Kothar and Liluri's education and training would prove to be invaluable.

As Liluri matured, her beauty began to attract the attention of city leaders who frequented the temple. They repeatedly questioned Ishtar about when Liluri would begin her duty as a priestess. They were already casting lots to see who would spend time with her first.

Those same men also reminded Ishtar that the time had come regarding Kothar. He would either need to join the other slave laborers constructing the wall, or if she intended to keep him in the temple, he would need to become a eunuch like Llisha. Ishtar, Ashima, and Llisha were all determined that Liluri and Kothar would not follow in their fate.

It was actually Liluri who first proposed a solution. They all knew the city leaders had two primary reasons for operating the temple to Asherah – and neither had anything to do with a religious conviction to worship the goddess. The first was for their own pleasure, and the second was for their personal financial gain. The offerings presented at the temple far exceeded the costs needed to maintain the temple and feed and house the priestesses and attendants. The receipts in excess of those costs ultimately lined the pockets of the city leaders.

"What if we are able to greatly increase the leaders' profits through an effort that Kothar and I lead?" Liluri asked. "Wouldn't their greed compel them to listen to our plan?"

They knew the leaders of Jericho were not morally upstanding men. They would be more than willing to turn a blind eye if they knew it would bring them financial gain. Quickly a plan unfolded.

∽

8

THE POWER OF KNOWLEDGE.

~

"What if the temple was to take over the city's inn?" Liluri proposed.

"The inn located along the city's eastern wall has fourteen sleeping rooms and a pantry for preparing meals," Kothar added. "Some of those rooms could still be used as lodging for visitors, but the majority could be used as additional rooms for the worship of Asherah with the priestesses. We could more than double the profits of the temple, which should please the city leaders."

"And," Liluri continued, "since lodgers in the inn would on occasion include married couples, who would be better to oversee the inn than a husband and wife?"

"And who would that husband and wife be?" Ishtar asked, already knowing the answer.

"It would be Kothar and me! I could serve as your second at the inn, and Kothar could be the master over the attendants just as Llisha is here in the temple."

"Do you not think the city leaders will see through the thin veil of your scheme?" Ishtar asked.

Ashima provided the answer before anyone else could speak. "Your powers of persuasion and influence, chief priestess, will quickly convince them that their long-term profits will more than make up for the loss of satisfying their short-term lust!"

They all looked at one another and smiled, because they knew Ashima spoke the truth. The city leaders may have thought they managed the town, but the reality was that Ishtar, in many ways, oversaw them! Knowledge is power – and the chief priestess had a treasure trove overflowing with knowledge!

Over the next several days, Ishtar proposed the idea to the city leaders individually. Initially, each one was resistant. They all had their eye on what they intended to be their prize – Liluri. But when Ishtar reminded each of them of a secret they would never want disclosed, they quickly yielded to her way of thinking.

After Ishtar visited each one, the city leaders met as a group to consider the proposal. It came as little surprise that the proposal was unanimously accepted with little discussion. Accordingly, Kothar and Liluri did not waste any time. Ishtar led them in a brief exchange of commitment to one another and declared them to be husband and wife. A wedding feast was promptly prepared for all of those in the temple. The couple consummated their marriage without delay, leaving no doubt they were truly husband and wife.

Trade at the inn prospered under Liluri's supervision. Her cleverness and cunning, combined with Kothar's watchful eye, quickly enabled the new enterprise to be a profitable success. They soon were making plans to increase the number of sleeping rooms in the inn by acquiring the shop and home of the tradesman next door. Liluri offered him a price that was much more than fair, and the tradesman readily accepted. Though the offer was generous, the increased profits would make up for it in no time.

Ishtar was pleased with Liluri's accomplishments and took every opportunity to express her pleasure whenever the two of them were together. Ishtar had known since Liluri was a child that she would one day rise to become her successor – and the city leaders soon began to concur.

It was a position, however, Liluri was in no hurry to assume. Her bond with Ishtar had in many ways become even stronger than the bond with her mother. Even Ashima had witnessed it over the years. But she did so without any jealousy or regret. Ashima desired the best for her daughter, and she knew Ishtar was able to help her achieve it.

The night before Liluri turned thirty-two years old, Llisha arrived at the inn with an urgent message for her to accompany him back to the temple. Ishtar was ill, and she was calling for Liluri to come quickly.

"I had hoped we would still have more time together," the chief priestess said, as she struggled to breathe. Liluri had seen her only two days before, and there had been no indication she was ill.

Ishtar continued with great effort. "It appears the goddess Asherah has decided it is my time to die, and there is nothing more anyone can do." She looked disapprovingly at the soothsayers and magicians who were standing around her as she spoke.

"It is of utmost importance that I name my successor before I die so the temple can continue to function without any disruption," she said, gasping for air. "It is no secret that you are the one I have chosen to follow me as chief priestess, and now we must make it official. I have informed the city leaders and they are all in agreement with my selection. So, in the presence of these witnesses, I hereby declare you will become chief priestess upon my death!"

Immediately, she dismissed everyone who had witnessed her proclamation, and Liluri and Ishtar were left to exchange their final words – including the passing of secrets. Those secrets, which had aways been the chief priestess's source of her power, were now being guarded by my mother.

"I know you are still young," Ishtar told my mother, "but you have shown you are ready. And now with this additional knowledge I have passed on to you, you will be able to lead with great power. However, I must caution you. Do not ever drop your guard! If you do, the leaders of our city – including the king – will try and control you. You must never let them. You are more cunning than the whole lot of them – use that! And never let them see any weakness in you!"

The two women spoke a short while longer until Ishtar had no more strength. She lay down her head and immediately fell asleep. It was a sleep that would never end. Within a matter of minutes, her breathing stopped … and my mother became the new chief priestess.

～

9

AN AUDIENCE WITH THE KING

〜

*W*hen King Arsu learned that Liluri was now the chief priestess, he immediately summoned her to the palace. Though her mother had been a frequent visitor to the palace, Liluri had never entered its doors.

Ashima told her daughter what she might expect. But Ashima had never gone to the palace as the chief priestess, only as the king's priestess, so she was not certain how Liluri would be received.

Liluri realized she was about to meet her biological father for the first time. If he knew she was his daughter, he had never attempted to make any contact. He had probably viewed her as an inconvenience during her mother's final weeks of pregnancy when Ashima was unable to serve him. But then again, Liluri wasn't even sure the king knew she was Ashima's daughter.

Liluri did her best not to be intimidated by her surroundings as she was led into the king's meeting chambers. Ishtar's final words kept echoing in her mind: "You have great power. Don't ever drop your guard. Because if you do, the king will try to control you."

She was surprised to find the king alone in the room. "Welcome to the palace, chief priestess," King Arsu greeted her. "You are as young and as lovely as I have heard. Though Ishtar remained lovely into her old age, there is no denying that the luster had disappeared from the rose. It is wonderful to see that the luster has returned!"

"I am honored Ishtar chose me to follow in her footsteps, my king," Liluri interrupted. "Her beauty and wisdom were without peer, as I'm sure the king will agree."

"Spoken like a true chief priestess," the king acknowledged as he resumed control of the conversation. "It's just that as I look into your eyes, I see your mother, whose beauty I once held in the highest esteem. She was barely more than a child herself when she and I first … met. How is Ashima these days?"

"She is well," Liluri replied. "Thank you for asking. But I imagine my king wants to hear the new chief priestess's assurance that the temple and inn will continue to function as efficiently as when Ishtar was in the role. And, that the worship needs of the city's men will continue to be tended to by the priestesses – and the income derived from that worship will continue to increase. I can assure you that will be the case, as I follow in the path Ishtar has set before me."

"Well, thank you, my dear, for your assurance," the king responded. "But I would expect no less. Your longevity in the role of chief priestess depends upon your favorable performance!

"No, I have simply called you here because I want you and I to have a close relationship so you will keep me fully informed. Ishtar kept her secrets from me, and I have no intention of allowing you to do the same.

She had already been in her position for many years by the time I became king; she had power over me. But that won't be the case with you, will it? After all, you would never do anything against your king … or your father?"

Arsu saw Liluri's look of surprise, and he knew he had the upper hand – at least for the moment. "Yes, I am well aware you are my daughter," he continued. "Though no one else will ever know, you and I will. And we will share that unique bond and affection that Ishtar and I never could. As a matter of fact, come and embrace your father."

Liluri did not move. She was surprised by the king's confession that he was her father. She also did not want to show weakness by succumbing to his command. But the king would not stand down. "Your king has commanded you to come here and give me an embrace. Does our new chief priestess not believe she needs to obey her king?"

Ishtar had not told her any secrets she could use now to keep from obeying the king. If she disobeyed, he could have her taken to the dungeon and stripped of her position. Hesitantly, she approached the king and the two embraced.

"That is more like it," the king said. "This will be our little secret that only we share. Your mother and I enjoyed great satisfaction in worshiping the goddess Asherah together. And now through the union she and I enjoyed, I can do so once more – with you!"

Liluri stared in horror as she realized what the king meant. As she tried to back away, he used his strength to overpower her. "But I am a married woman," she pleaded. "I know you are, and I am a married man," he replied. "But I am also your king, and we will lie here and worship the goddess Asherah together!"

She attempted to call out, but he quickly restrained her. "You are in my chambers today," he said, with no hint of compassion. "No one will come to your aid. We will enjoy this moment together, and then you will return to the temple and perform your duties as chief priestess until I summon you to return!"

The act was over in a few minutes, but my mother knew its impact would last a lifetime. The king hastily left, and she sat alone in the chamber trying to compose herself. Her position as chief priestess and, more importantly, as a woman had been violated by not only her king ... but also by her father.

Outrage, shame, fear, and grief overwhelmed her. As she made her way back to the temple, she considered what to do next. There wasn't a higher authority she could go to about the king's actions. He *was* the highest authority in the land. Liluri also didn't feel she could tell Kothar, her mother, or anyone else.

This would be one of the secrets she would keep – at least for now. She immediately began to think about how she would respond the next time the king summoned her.

~

10

UNEXPECTED NEWS

❧

*D*espite her pain and turmoil, my mother returned to the temple without letting anyone know what had occurred. She carried out her responsibilities flawlessly in the weeks that followed. Temple priestesses, attendants, and patrons lauded her for the way she had assumed Ishtar's role with such proficiency.

But in her heart, she was haunted by the memory of what the king had done to her . . . and by the fear of what he might do again. One afternoon, six weeks after that fateful day, a messenger arrived from the palace. He insisted to the temple attendants that he had been instructed by the king to deliver his message to the chief priestess in person.

Though Liluri's expression was stoic as she received the messenger, inside she was trembling. "What message does King Arsu send me?" she demanded of the messenger.

"Chief priestess, the message is not from King Arsu," the messenger replied. "I have been sent by King Aleyin to tell you his father is dead. He died just a short while ago, and Aleyin has assumed his place as the heir to the king. King Aleyin asks that you lead your priestesses to tend to the grief and confusion his father's death will cause the men of our city. He assures you the work of the temple priestesses will continue to be held in the highest regard under his reign. He looks forward to telling you in person in the weeks ahead."

Liluri could not believe her ears. Though outwardly she feigned an expression of sadness and concern, inwardly she couldn't help but be overjoyed. The man who had caused her such great pain was dead. He would no longer be a threat to her! And she would never place herself in the position to be harmed in any way by his son – her half-brother.

"Please convey my condolences to the king," she replied to the messenger. "And assure him that the priestesses and I, as well as all our attendants, will do everything in our power to assuage the grief that will result from this news. Assure him of my steadfast support as he assumes his position as my king. And that I, too, look forward to telling him in person when he has the opportunity."

Though Aleyin had been greatly mistaken about how she would receive the news of their father's death, he had been correct regarding the grief that many in the city would feel. Over the next several weeks, the temple had many more visits than usual. The city leaders were secretly elated by the financial gain they gleaned from the king's demise.

A few days after Arsu's death, Liluri began to feel ill. Though she knew it had nothing to do with his death, she soon realized it had everything to do with him! Though the gods had never seen fit to bless her and Kothar with children, she suddenly realized she was expecting a child.

She decided that no one would ever be the wiser – not Kothar, her mother, or anyone else. Kothar would rejoice at the news that he was soon to be a father. She would never tell him anything to the contrary. She determined that the secret had died with Arsu, and never again would she allow herself to be subject to the control of another person!

Several weeks later, some additional unexpected news arrived in the city. At the time, no one anticipated how the news might have anything to do with the people of Jericho, but it was surprising, nonetheless. It had been over sixty years since the kings of Egypt had troubled the lands of Canaan. Their armies had long ago vacated our lands and returned to Egypt. But the might of their army had remained a fear even to that day.

Gratefully their king, Thutmose II, just like his father and grandfather before him, had shown little interest in our lands, so we had lived in relative peace. Still, work on our walls had continued for almost 100 years.

The surprising news that day was that the mighty army of Egypt had been summarily defeated and destroyed. Apparently, Thutmose II had led the Egyptian warriors to recapture a nation of slaves that he had freed only a few days earlier. Even though the slaves numbered close to 2 million adults and children, it was not their force that had defeated the Egyptians.

The slaves, who called themselves Israelites, had no weaponry. They had no chariots or horses bred for battle. They had very little with which to defend themselves. Apparently, the Egyptian army came upon them with full force, and the Israelites were cut off from escaping by the Red Sea. The result should have been predictable.

But the messengers told us the God of the Israelites had parted the sea so the people could cross over to the eastern shore. While they did so, He kept the Egyptian army at bay through what was described as a wall of fire. When the Israelites were safely across the dry seabed, the wall of fire disappeared and the Egyptians resumed their chase.

As the Egyptian army charged through the parted sea, the God of the Israelites caused the waters to come back together, completely submerging the warriors, their chariots, and their horses. We were told that none of the Egyptians survived, not even King Thutmose II, who had been leading the charge.

The enemy we had once feared – the Egyptian army – no longer existed. And the Israelites did not appear to be a fighting force to be feared . . . but their God most certainly did. King Aleyin announced that our spies would keep a watchful eye on them, and we would continue the work on our walls … just in case.

All their lives, the people of Jericho had worshiped the gods – most notably Baal and Asherah. But never had any of those gods demonstrated such power. Yes, the magicians taught that Baal had sent the flood waters out of his anger, and Asherah had restored life. But there were some who attributed those things to the God of the Israelites, who were also descendants of Noah through his son Shem.

And now, with the news of what had happened to the Egyptians, our people began to fear the God of the Israelites.

∼

11

A NEW BEGINNING AND AN END

~

*M*y first cry echoed throughout the temple on a cool autumn evening. My grandmother, Ashima, remained by my mother's side acting as her midwife. Llisha and my father were there to fret and add any support my grandmother would permit.

Though Llisha and my grandmother had never been able to marry, the love they shared had never diminished. Since Ishtar's death, my grandmother and Llisha had loyally stayed by each other's side, serving my mother as her assistants in the temple. My father continued to oversee the attendants at the inn, and my mother oversaw them all, as well as the growing number of priestesses. She worked right up until the evening I was born, then returned to her duties two days later, despite my grandmother's objections.

As a result, my grandmother and Llisha took responsibility for my care whenever my mother was attending to her duties. As the second generation of our family was now growing up in the temple, the surroundings and routine felt normal to everyone.

From the time I was a baby, I was told I looked like my mother's identical twin. I never gave it much thought in those early years. Liluri is a very attractive woman, so I was honored by the compliment. But somehow Llisha surmised who my real father was while I was still a newborn, even though no one else did – including Kothar. Out of loyalty to my mother, though, Llisha never mentioned it to anyone, not even my grandmother.

Soon after I was born, King Aleyin and the city leaders received additional news about the Israelites. After their miraculous rescue at the Red Sea, the Israelites congregated in the wilderness surrounding Mt. Sinai for many months. It was hard to imagine why any group would choose to remain in that foreboding place, but the longer they stayed there, the more our people's fear of them diminished.

But those concerns reignited the day the Israelites started traveling north-ward out of the peninsula toward Canaan. Our leaders were informed they weren't coming here to live among us or settle in the uninhabited lands. Their God had told them He was giving them a land flowing with milk and honey. He was giving them our land and our cities!

Though our walls were already well fortified, the work had not yet been completed. In order to complete the work before the Israelites arrived, the king and his council decided to double the number of workers. Every male servant, regardless of age, was now tasked with working on the walls. Every male attendant working in the temple and the inn, including my father and Llisha, was conscripted into the effort. Despite her influence, my mother was unsuccessful in having Llisha exempted from the work in light of his old age and declining health. She was told no exceptions would be made.

The walls were finally finished on my eighth birthday, ushering in the era that we were now the most fortified city in Canaan providing defense against any enemy. The walls were a marvel of engineering and effort, and no other city was protected in such a way. The city leaders boasted that even the gods would be powerless against the defenses of our walls.

Five generations had invested their lives to see the walls completed, and during those 108 years, countless lives had been lost or spent in the process. Llisha was among those whose physical strength and health had been depleted by the work. Each day he valiantly labored despite his diminishing state.

When King Aleyin boasted upon completion that his great-great-grandfather Malakbel had begun the work, Llisha proudly reminded everyone that Malakbel was *his* great-grandfather as well. Llisha's grandfather and father had contributed to the work – perhaps not as kings – but as valiant laborers. And now he, too, had helped finish what they had labored to build.

The men who worked by Llisha's side no longer viewed him as the son of a traitor or the eunuch who worked in the temple; rather, they had come to see him as a man of integrity. He had restored honor to his family name – honor that had been unjustly taken.

Even as a young girl, I was proud of him. And since he was the only grandfather I would ever know, I was delighted to be part of his family. I also was proud of the honorable legacy that extended back through my grandfather's ancestors. It was then I realized I was not one of lesser birth than the king, I was his equal, and I forever would be. I would never lower my view of myself or my sights for the future again.

Toward the end of Llisha's labor, it was all he could do to walk each day to the wall. He never complained and never sought to be excused from his work. His commitment, despite his infirmities, was an inspiration to the other men.

During the final days, the taskmasters supervising the wall construction and the men working alongside Llisha did everything they could to lighten his load. When the work was finished, Llisha returned to the temple, but he never regained his strength. He lived out the remainder of his days confined to a bed.

The king declared a seven-day feast as the city celebrated the completion of the walls. Animals were sacrificed throughout the week on the altars to Baal as a thanksgiving offering for his favor in finishing the work. The rooms in the temple and inn were filled day and night as men came to join with the priestesses in expressing their worship to Asherah.

Any fear the citizens of Jericho had regarding the Israelites had now completely vanished. Our walls were in place. No one would ever prevail against us!

～

12

THE FOURTH GENERATION

~

*D*uring the months that passed after the celebration, I spent as much time as I could with Llisha. I wanted to learn everything I could about his family, and I wanted to know as much as I could about my heritage. The more I learned, the more my hatred grew for the kings of Jericho. Though Aleyin had not been a party to any of the actions against Llisha and his parents, he had never done anything to redeem himself in my eyes, so I considered him just as guilty as the rest.

When I was eleven years old, I made a vow to Llisha. "I promise I will fully restore all that was taken from you and your family. Your honor has already been restored in the eyes of the citizens of Jericho, but I will not rest until Aleyin acknowledges what his father and grandfather did to you and your parents. I will rebuild your family's fortune and standing."

"Granddaughter," Llisha replied, "one of the happiest days of my life was the day you were born. You and your mother have brought a joy and peace to my life that is greater than anything ever taken from me. Though neither of you is the product of my seed, I have always thought of you both as my own flesh and blood. Do not waste your life trying to undo things you cannot change; rather, invest your life in building a joyful and prosperous future."

His statement gave me the courage to ask a question I had never voiced before. "Grandfather, from whose seed did my mother come?"

"Rahab, that is not for me to say," he replied. "That is a question you need to ask your mother."

"I have tried, but she refuses to tell me," I countered. "I know Grandmother was once the priestess to King Arsu. Was it his seed from which my mother was conceived? Does my bloodline go back through him to Malakbel just like yours? You are part of the third generation that came after him. Is my mother part of the fourth generation through Arsu?"

Llisha gave me an empathetic look. "I will answer your question because I believe you need to know. But you must never tell your mother or grandmother that I have told you. If they ever choose to do so, they must believe you are hearing the news for the first time. Will you make that promise to me?"

"Yes, I will, Grandfather," I responded.

He stared into my eyes for a moment to ensure I was sincere in my promise. "Yes, your mother was conceived from the seed of Arsu," he answered.

"Then that makes me part of the fifth generation from Malakbel just like Aleyin's offspring, doesn't it, Grandfather?"

But Llisha didn't answer me. When I looked into his eyes, I knew there was something he was not telling me. So I repeated my question.

"No, it does not," he replied softly. "Because you, too, are from the seed of Arsu."

"How can that be?" I implored. "How can my biological grandfather also be my biological father?"

Llisha remained silent as he considered his next words carefully. "Your grandmother chose to be the priestess to the king so that I might be freed from the dungeon. She sacrificed that part of herself for me. Your mother was a blessing from the goddess Asherah to your grandmother for her act of sacrifice. But your conception came about in a different way.

"I am only telling you this because you need to know. There are only two people who know the truth – your mother and me. Your father and your grandmother do not even know, and you must never tell them."

"How is it that you know these things, and my father and grandmother do not?"

"Because I saw it in you from the moment you were born," Llisha replied. "And the night after your birth, your mother unintentionally confided in me. When I looked in on her to see if she needed anything, she was looking at you as she held you in her arms. But I could see she was troubled.

"I told her the only way she could be freed from her burden was to share it with someone. When she argued that she could not share this burden with anyone, I told her she could share it with me.

"'It concerns this precious little baby I hold in my arms,' she said. 'I must protect her from ever having to experience what I have endured.'

"'I will do everything I can to protect her as I have endeavored to protect you,' I said.

"'Yes, I know you will try,' she replied, 'but you weren't able to protect me from this – or from him!'

"At that moment, the tears she had kept hidden for nine months were unleashed. And suddenly her secret spilled out to me with those tears. She told me how she had been summoned for an audience with the king soon after she had been appointed chief priestess. She explained how King Arsu had raped her that night to demonstrate his power over her – even though he knew she was his biological daughter.

"She went on to tell me that she was wrestling with the fact that the most precious gift she had ever received – you – was the result of the most horrific act ever perpetrated against her.

"If Arsu had still been living," Llisha confided, "I would have marched over to the palace and killed the king for what he had done to your mother. But I kept my emotions in check and reminded her that the gods had already extracted revenge – they had taken Arsu's life just a few short weeks after he assaulted her. 'Trust the justice of the gods and do not continue to torment yourself about the one who defiled you; rather, focus on the precious gift you have been given instead, and trust the gods to protect her in the future.'"

We sat in silence as I thought about what Llisha had just told me. His words had not shocked me; rather, they had only proved what I had long suspected. "That means that I, too, am part of the fourth generation from Malakbel – and King Aleyin is my half-brother.

"Llisha, I promise you," I said, "I will take your words to my grave. I will not betray your confidence. And I will restore all that has been taken from you – and all that was done to each and every one of you!"

13

WORTHY OF A KING

~

*L*lisha died three weeks later. I was never certain whether our conversation took place because he knew he was about to die and didn't want those secrets buried with him, or because it was ordained by the fates. Regardless, I was grateful he had not passed before telling me the truth.

The priestesses and attendants in the temple and the inn are like family. As chief priestess, my mother is the matriarch. Everyone looks to her for guidance and direction. But Llisha had been the patriarch. He rose to that role as a result of his character and compassion. He was my grandmother's lifelong friend and companion, though they had been robbed of the joy of marrying. To me, Llisha was always my grandfather.

But the same was true for all who grew up in the temple. He had always been there to encourage every one of us whenever we needed it – and to correct us whenever we needed that as well.

That was particularly true for my friend, Chusor. He was two years younger than I was. His mother, Talaya, had been the priestess to King Aleyin at the time of Chusor's conception. So it was reasonable to assume he was the half-brother of Aleyin's legitimate sons and daughters. But then again, most of us were half-brothers or half-sisters to someone's legitimate family. Perhaps that was one of the greatest bonds we shared.

From the time he could walk, Chusor was Llisha's constant companion and often imitated Llisha's expressions and mannerisms. Llisha never tired of Chusor's endless questions, and he often stooped down to Chusor's level so he could look him in the eye as he answered. Though Llisha's death affected all of us, it hit Chusor especially hard.

My mother was aware King Aleyin's permission was needed for Llisha's body to be buried with honor in the tomb of his grandfather, Shachar. She also knew the king would more than likely withhold his approval since kings Arsu and Attar had branded Llisha the son of a traitor. Thus, she knew a direct request to the king would be fruitless.

However, King Aleyin had recently named his childhood ally, Chemosh, as his new king's counselor. The counselor's authority was exceeded only by that of the king himself, and my mother was confident he would have the authority to grant her request.

She also knew Chemosh was a frequent visitor to the temple, having shown great interest in Chusor's mother, Talaya, once she was no longer serving as the priestess to the king. On more than one occasion, Chemosh had confided information to Talaya that my mother knew would displease the king should he find out.

My mother had become proficient at gathering secrets and using them to accomplish her wishes. I was incredibly proud of her position and power. When she confronted Chemosh, he became more than obliging. Once Chemosh granted his approval, arrangements were made for Llisha's body to be interred in Shachar's burial vault. It was located in one of the natural caves situated in the hills to the north of the city.

The attendants in the temple prepared his body for burial while my mother arranged to have offerings prepared to be buried with his body. Once preparations were completed, the procession began. It was led by several soothsayers and magicians whose job was to frighten away the evil spirits. Immediately behind them were several paid mourners and then the funeral bier on which Llisha's body rested, carried by six temple attendants. My grandmother, mother, father, and I stoically walked behind the bier. A large procession followed us – including all the priestesses and attendants – as well as a large number of men who had worked alongside Llisha on the wall. It was a procession worthy of a king!

When we arrived at the burial site, the stone covering the entry to the vault was rolled away. The first men to enter the tomb carefully displaced the remains of a previous body in order to make room for Llisha. They were followed by men carrying offering jars containing grain, wine, and oil, together with a sack of clothing – all items Llisha would need as he made his journey through the netherworld. Though I did not enter the tomb, I could see a jumble of bones scattered around the periphery of the vault together with the remains of previous offerings. Apparently, those offerings had exceeded what Llisha's ancestors required for their respective journeys – or so I thought at the time.

Once his body was laid in the vault, the procession began making its way back to the temple. The stone made a loud thud as the men rolled it back over the opening, and it settled into the indentation in the ground. For some reason that sound signaled the finality of Llisha's life to me, and the tears I had successfully held back were unleashed with a vengeance. My grandmother, mother, and I returned to our private chambers in the temple to grieve privately while the rest of the mourners partook of the funeral meal.

As the days passed, I was satisfied we had honored my grandfather well in his death. But I was now even more committed to making the kings pay for what they had taken from his family.

Llisha's passing cast a pall over our lives for the next several weeks until it was washed away by a joyous announcement. "Rahab, your father and I are expecting another child!" my mother happily declared. "I had resigned myself that Asherah had determined I would have no more children after you – but that has changed! Your father is certain he will soon have a son."

"We already have a perfect daughter," my father interrupted. "Now it is only fitting that we should have a perfect son as well!"

Our entire temple family celebrated the news. Llisha, my grandmother, my mother, my father, and I – for my first twelve years – had been only children. But now I was to have a brother or a sister, and I couldn't have been happier! Seven months later my brother, Elyon, was born! My father was beside himself with joy.

And three years later, the gods again smiled upon my parents when Rimmon was born. My father now had two sons!

∾

14

A NEW PRIEST AND A NEW PRIESTESS

⁓

The week before Rimmon's first birthday, my mother was summoned to meet with King Aleyin. He had just returned from his visit to Hazor to meet with their King Jabin. Aleyin was attempting to build a stronger alliance among the Canaanite kings. He knew if he could convince Jabin to join the alliance, the other northern kings would do so as well.

As she entered Aleyin's meeting hall, my mother was surprised to see Chemosh and another man she did not recognize. The king promptly began to recount his visit to Hazor to my mother.

"Chief Priestess," Aleyin began, "I was greatly impressed with the city of Hazor. It is the fortress city for the northern kingdoms of Canaan, just as Jericho is for the eastern kingdoms. It is slightly larger than our city, but its walls pale in comparison to ours. However, its most striking characteristic is its temple.

"It is twice the size of ours and its décor and furnishings promote heartfelt worship for Asherah. One can immediately sense how she must be pleased by the offerings of pleasure being presented to her there. My time in their temple has inspired me to see how we might make changes to ours in order to promote greater ecstatic worship.

"Counselor Chemosh and I were so inspired that I decided to invite one of the priests of their temple to come to Jericho with us so he might help us make similar improvements. Liluri, allow me to introduce Priest Mawat to you."

Mawat took my mother's hand and said, "It is such an honor to meet you, Chief Priestess. Your king and his counselor have told me so much about you. But I must tell you that their words were not able to adequately express your beauty and charm."

My mother slowly withdrew her hand as she replied, "Well, I am certain they were gracious in their praise as they always are." As she looked at the king and Chemosh, she quickly surmised their intentions.

They had become fearful of her. They knew the secrets she possessed could bring about their downfall if she so chose. Chemosh's recent experience over the burial of Llisha had helped convince him of that truth. My mother had a good idea what the king was going to say next.

"I have invited Mawat to assume the position in our temple of chief priest. I know that position has never existed before within our temple. A chief priestess has always held the position of authority – you and those who served before you performing so remarkably.

"And as chief priestess, you will continue to oversee the priestesses just as you always have," the king continued. "But Mawat will become the ultimate authority over all who serve in the temple – including you. I have charged him with the responsibility of leading our temple to rival and surpass that which I witnessed in Hazor. On a more personal note, I am also mindful of an added benefit for you. With him assuming some of your responsibilities, you will be freed up to attend to the growing needs of your family. I am sure you would be grateful to have that added time."

"King Aleyin, you are so kind to think of me and my family, but doesn't a change of this nature require approval of the full council?" my mother inquired.

"Oh, I am certain they will fully embrace my recommendation," the king answered, as he nodded and smiled at the two men.

My mother knew there was nothing she could do at the moment to change the course of this discussion. She had not anticipated this maneuver on the part of the king or his counselor. She would need to thoughtfully consider her next move.

"Liluri," the king continued, "might I suggest Mawat accompany you to the temple and the inn so you can introduce him to the priestesses and attendants as together you announce this exciting news? I know you will give him your complete support, just as you have always given it to me. And I look forward to seeing how Asherah leads him to direct the activities of our temple to even greater heights of worship."

Chemosh made no attempt to disguise his delight as my mother walked past him to exit the hall. But then again, neither did the priestesses and attendants attempt to hide their displeasure when she introduced Mawat and his new role. The staff was acutely aware this was retaliation against my mother for the way we had honored Llisha in burial. It was a reminder to us the king and his counselor would always hold tight control over us.

One of Mawat's first directives was that priestesses and attendants could not divulge any worshipers' secrets to anyone other than himself. Any staff member who disobeyed would have her or his tongue cut out. "The men who come to worship should feel assured that no one knows of their indiscretions other than their priest – whose duty it is to bring them before Asherah," he said behind a mask of piety. The workers knew the only thing that had changed was who would now hold the power of the secrets.

Another change he made was to name his servant, whom he brought from Hazor, as the new chief attendant of the inn. Mawat made an insincere announcement of how my father had served in that capacity with distinction, and it was time for him to be rewarded for his efforts and excused from his day-to-day responsibilities. My father would still be available to provide counsel to the new chief attendant, but otherwise he would have no authority.

There was no question that my parents were being stripped of their power. And we all knew the "unholy three" – as we began to refer to the king, Chemosh, and Mawat – would not be satisfied until my parents were completely disgraced and humiliated – so great was the fear and offense felt by the king over Llisha's honorable burial.

As I watched the collapse of my parents' standing, I began to doubt whether I could fulfill my promise to Llisha to restore his family's reputation and position. That thought weighed heavily on me on the eve of my sixteenth birthday. The next day, I would officially become a priestess. Though I was still the chief priestess's daughter, I no longer enjoyed the privilege that position once afforded me. I had noticed Mawat's lecherous looks at me since the first day I met him. I feared what the next day would bring – and whether or not my mother would be powerless to do anything about it.

∾

15

THE PRIESTESS TO THE PRINCE

~

S oon after the day had dawned, my mother presented me to Asherah as the newest priestess in the temple. All of the priestesses surrounded me as my mother presided over the ceremony, just as she had done so many times before. However, this was the first time the novice priestess was her daughter, and her heart was heavy. Though she and I had grown up in this life, she had wanted something better for me. Unfortunately, she didn't know how to achieve it – particularly now that her authority had been compromised.

Mawat watched the ceremony from a distance. I was thankful that this part of my mother's responsibilities had not yet been stripped from her. When the ceremony concluded, Mawat approached my mother and me and told us the chief priest should be the first to introduce me to my role as priestess. His not-so-subtle smile betrayed the fact he had been planning this for quite a while – perhaps since the first day he saw me.

However, my mother interrupted him. "Chief Priest, that is so selfless and pious of you to offer to introduce her to her duties. And I am certain it would be a great honor for Rahab. But I have just received a message from the palace that King Aleyin has called for her. She is to make her way to the palace with haste."

Mawat was indignant. "I received no such message!"

My mother replied demurely, "I am certain the king intended for both of us to receive his message. His messenger awaits Rahab at the door if you would like to inquire of him yourself. Apparently, he is waiting to accompany her to the palace."

This response obviously flustered Mawat. He could ill-afford to ignore the king's command. I wasn't fully sure what was taking place, but one glance at my mother told me she was up to something.

"Rahab, you mustn't keep the king waiting," the chief priestess urged. "Make haste and go join the messenger, and accompany him to the palace."

"I will," I replied, as I turned and walked away from the chief priest, who was looking quite incredulous … and my mother, who was looking quite victorious!

When I arrived at the temple's door, I was surprised to find the king's eldest son, Prince Lotan, awaiting me. The prince was actually two years younger than I was, so according to our laws he was not yet permitted to enter the temple. He was required to wait at the door despite his rank. I had seen him at official ceremonies over the years, but I had never actually spoken to him.

"Are you surprised to see me here?" he asked.

"To be perfectly honest, I am surprised," I responded. "How is it that your father sent you to get me?"

"Well, it was actually my idea," he answered with a grin. "I have admired you from afar for some time. Apparently, your mother took notice of my lingering gazes of admiration. She encountered me on the palace grounds last week and told me today was when you were to begin your official duties as a priestess. She also confided that much older men had designs on you, and she feared for your safety.

"When I expressed concern, she told me there was nothing she could do. 'Only a request from the king could change her fate,' she said. So I told her, 'Then that is what will happen. I will ask my father to send for her, so she and I can spend the days together walking through the countryside, and she can get out from behind these walls.'

"So that is why I am here, Rahab. You and I are going out for a walk in the hills, and no one will disturb us because we do so with my father's blessings."

I couldn't help but smile. My mother had not lost her power – she had just learned how to use it in different ways!

Those walks became a daily occurrence, and despite our difference in social station, Lotan and I developed an unlikely friendship. I was formally designated as a priestess to the palace, and specifically to the prince, which kept Mawat away from me. Though I was assigned to the prince, our relationship never became physical. He never treated me as if I was something to be used; rather, our relationship was one of respect and deepening friendship.

But we both knew this arrangement could not last forever. I knew when Lotan turned sixteen, he would be required to lay with a priestess as a rite of passage. And we knew our relationship could never be more than child-hood friends. Perhaps one day I would be commanded to be his priestess – but nothing more.

Though I knew this in my head, my heart fell deeply in love with him, and I was certain he felt the same. When he turned sixteen, he bravely went before his father and said he did not want to bed me as his priestess; rather, he wanted me to be his wife. As you can imagine, King Aleyin would not hear of his son marrying a slave – even a pretty one – and forbade him from ever seeing me again.

In order to ensure our relationship was completely severed, he instructed Mawat to take personal control of the situation. I was no longer under the king's protection. I was now at the mercy of Mawat, and there was nothing my mother or father could do about it. I never saw Lotan again after that day, except from a distance. The king had, in essence, made me Mawat's property to do with as he saw fit.

I will not go into graphic detail, but the first night Mawat lay with me, he violated me beyond anything I could describe. His handling of me was brutal and cruel. This treatment continued every night for several weeks. Each time he would remind me, "Asherah has answered my prayers. She has granted me the one possession that escaped me these past two years – she has granted me the satisfaction of worshiping her with you. May she be praised!"

Eventually, he became bored with me, and his violent treatment stopped. Another priestess caught his gaze. Though I was grateful to be released from his torture, I grieved for the priestesses who would follow me. Mawat released me to my mother's supervision, as he had with so many before me. But the damage had been done, and my soul was shattered.

I had many reasons to dislike the king, Chemosh, and Mawat. They had each humiliated my family. I knew them to be dishonorable and evil men, but now my dislike for them had become unadulterated hatred, and it grew with each passing day. I would find a way to free myself – and my family – from their bondage. And I would destroy them … if it was the last thing I did!

∾

16

FROM THE TEMPLE TO THE INN

~

For the next few months, my mother kept me close by her side as I recovered from the physical abuse inflicted by Mawat. She and I both knew it would take far longer to recover from the mental and emotional abuse I had suffered.

The only drawback to staying with my mother at the temple was I frequently saw Mawat. I was relieved, however, that he never attempted to make any contact with me – he just looked at me with disdain whenever he passed by. His obvious lack of remorse over what he had done caused me to hate him even more.

Once I had fully recovered from my physical injuries, I was fairly certain what my mother was going to say when she came to me one day, looking resolute. "As the chief priestess, it is time for me to put you to work, Rahab. You can't remain here in the temple with me if you are not fulfilling your duties as a priestess. I can't be seen as showing you favoritism.

"But as your mother, I do not want you to remain here in the temple where you will continually have to encounter Mawat. So, here is what I have decided. I need a priestess to take up residence at the inn and oversee the other priestesses on my behalf. I can no longer effectively do so in both places. I have been considering this assignment for some time, even before Mawat came into his role. And I cannot think of anyone better suited for it than you.

"However, there is one adjustment that must be made. Mawat's servant continues to disrupt the effective service of the attendants at the inn. We must devise a way to return unrestricted supervision to your father. You can then oversee the priestesses and the overall operation of the inn with your father's assistance.

You will be under my direct supervision, taking orders from no one except me. Mawat rarely visits the inn, but if he should do so and attempt to give you an order, you can tell him you will be more than happy to comply once you receive instructions from me. After all, the king made it clear that my supervision of the priestesses is to be unfettered.

"Quite frankly, the overall function of the inn and our service to our worshipers and guests there have suffered since Mawat's servant arrived. Once we eliminate him, I expect you to oversee the inn with a firm hand. You will need to ensure our priestesses and attendants are treated well, but also that they are treating the worshipers and guests with the utmost care and attention they deserve."

"Mother, I am honored you have chosen me for this role," I responded, "and I will not let you down. I am certain Mawat's servant will be gone within the week!"

"Rahab, I knew you would rise to the occasion. In many ways I have been training you for this responsibility all your life, and I know you are just the person I need in this role."

Later that day, my mother introduced my new role to the inn staff. With the exception of Mawat's servant, they all affirmed her selection and assured me of their loyalty.

I had become suspicious that Mawat's servant was stealing money collected at the inn and passing it along to Mawat. Though I couldn't prove Mawat's involvement, I quickly gathered enough evidence to confirm the servant's guilt. But I knew in order to confront him, I would need the support of some of our council members who frequented the inn. It wasn't difficult to convince two of them once I showed them how the servant was stealing the offerings, and, in so doing, stealing the profits they would otherwise receive.

On the fourth day in my new role, I asked my mother to come to the inn and to bring Mawat. When they arrived, I asked Mawat's servant to join us and then proceeded to confront him. Before he could even attempt to deny my charges, the two councilmen joined us on my cue and confirmed the accusation. Mawat was left with no choice but to feign shock before he dispatched his servant to the dungeon for crimes against the city.

The servant's feet were barely out the door when I recommended my father be restored to his supervisory role. The councilmen wholeheartedly added their support to my suggestion. Mawat had learned early in his career how to read a room, so he, too, immediately supported my recommendation. However, I knew he would be looking for ways to retaliate for what I had just done. I had clearly won the day, and he was apparently content to take the loss – at least for now.

I wasted no time in gathering suggestions from the priestesses and attendants about how we might better serve those who came to the inn. With my mother's approval, we implemented many of those suggestions quickly. Within a month, guests and regular worshipers began commenting about how we had improved their experience. Our priestesses and attendants became even more committed to making further improvements.

Within sixty days, the inn was showing a significant increase in profits, which pleased the council to no end. Mawat, of course, took credit for all of the changes, including the decision to place me in my new role. But that also gave me assurance he would not attempt to retaliate against me.

As the years passed and I became more confident in my role, I began to explore my larger plan. If I was going to destroy the unholy trinity of Aleyin, Chemosh, and Mawat, it was time to take action. To formulate an effective plan, I needed to know everything possible about those men, their secrets, and their vulnerabilities.

Just before she died, my grandmother, Ashima, reminded me of the power of the secrets learned in the bed chambers. "But, Grandmother," I implored, "Mawat has threatened great harm to those who disclose a secret to anyone but him. The priestesses and attendants are fearful to do anything to the contrary."

"Of course they are, my dear," my grandmother replied weakly. "He knows they are fearful – so use that to your advantage. The priestesses all trust you and your mother. Tell them to pass along the less important secrets to Mawat, and to keep those that will help ensure the safety of those who serve in the temple and inn. Don't ever let him know what *you* know until the moment his destruction is assured. Until then, he will be none the wiser."

But I also knew I needed access to information that would never make its way to the bed chambers. I needed eyes and ears around the city. My childhood friend and companion, Chusor, became my greatest ally in gleaning that kind of information. He hated the chief counselor as much as I did. His mother, Talaya, had died soon after my grandmother due to a disease she had contracted from Chemosh. The man had shown no regret and no care for her. He had simply cast her out of his presence and left her to fend for herself.

Since his mother's death, Chusor had become engaged in a black market that was thriving in the city. It was a way for citizens of Jericho to buy and sell without being taxed by the king. In order to survive, the network needed to stay one step ahead of the king and the city leaders. This meant they were already listening for information that would aid their cause. Chusor had no reluctance about relaying that information to me. That way, nothing would ever be traced back to me.

I was soon privy to all the details of the unholy three's lives, including their comings and goings, and their conversations behind closed doors. This went on for months, and those months turned into years.

Chusor came to me one day with this report: "The Israelites have set up camp on the eastern shore of the Jordan River, which is at flood stage. But one of the councilmen asked Chemosh if it was possible for the Israelites' God to divide the waters of the river just like He parted the Red Sea. If that were to happen, everyone in that room knew the Israelites could be right outside our gates within a matter of days.

"And the council knows that if the God of the Israelites is leading them to occupy Canaan, Jericho will be the first city they attack. Aleyin continued to remind everyone of the strength of our walls. But the council asked Aleyin to again try rallying the other cities of Canaan to join forces to attack the Israelites rather than waiting for them to attack our cities one by one. 'If we sit back and do nothing, we will be greatly outmanned, regardless of the strength of our walls,' one of the council members said.

"Then Mawat added, 'And don't forget what their God did to the Egyptians, and even more recently to the Amorites on the east side of the Jordan.' One of the councilmen replied, 'Won't our god Baal fight for us, priest?' But the resounding answer from Mawat – and everyone else in the room – was silence!"

≈

17

TWO STRANGERS

∾

"*C*husor, if the Israelites are planning to attack our city, they will send spies to assess our defenses and our military strength," I reasoned. "Tell your most trusted men to watch for unknown travelers. They could come at any time, and I need to know of their arrival before Chemosh and the king!"

A few weeks later, Chusor came to the inn one afternoon to tell me two strangers had just set foot in Jericho. They appeared to be evaluating the strength and positioning of the walls from inside the city. Chusor's men were convinced the two were the Israelite spies we had been expecting.

I wanted to see the men for myself, so Chusor and I hastily made our way back to the city gates. I spotted the men as soon as we arrived, and I instantly knew they were Israelites. As I started toward them, I saw Chemosh approaching them from the opposite direction.

I moved closer to the spies and hid behind a merchant's cart so I could overhear their conversation with Chemosh. "Welcome to our city, travelers," Chemosh greeted them. "I am the chief counselor of the city. I don't believe I've seen the two of you here before. You look like foreigners. Where are you from?"

The older of the two men replied, "We are weary travelers from Moab on our way to Hebron. We have entered your city to find a place where we can rest for the night. We plan to continue our journey in the morning. Do you have any recommendations where we might find food and lodging for the night?"

Chemosh surprisingly did not challenge their answer, even though it was obvious they were not Moabites. Instead, he pointed them in the direction of the inn. I was relieved I had not tried to speak with them on the street. I would now have an opportunity to talk with them at the inn.

As I turned to head back to the inn, I heard Chemosh quietly talking to one of his guards. "I have directed those two men to the inn. Follow them and report back to me on what they do on their way there. Let me know if they stop to speak with anyone or look at anything along the way. But do not let them see you following them."

I wanted to speak to the strangers before Chemosh had any further contact, so I decided to delay the guard. I removed the pin from the wheel of the merchant's cart I was hiding behind. The wheel fell off and the cart's contents of pomegranates spilled and scattered in every direction. People ran to help the merchant gather his fruit, and Chemosh and the guard became distracted by the commotion.

Apparently, the two Israelite travelers had seen Chemosh dispatch the guard to follow them. So, they took advantage of my disruption and briskly made their way down a different walkway from the one Chemosh had pointed out.

I cut through an alley and intercepted them along their route. "Well, you two look like you need help finding your way. Follow me to my inn where you can rest and refresh yourselves from your travels." The two men followed without any hesitation. It was as if they knew they could trust me.

After the two foreigners, Iru and Elah, were settled and had eaten their meal, I approached their table. "Gentlemen, it is obvious you are not Moabites, but rather you are Israelites. Please do not fear me. I mean you no harm.

"Instead, I believe we can be allies. All of us in Canaan are aware of how your God has gone before your people, defeating the Egyptians by drowning them in the sea. We have heard how he defeated King Sihon of the Amorites and King Og of Bashan. We know not a single survivor remained in those lands after your people came to occupy them.

"Such is the fear in Jericho. We are afraid your God will destroy us all. It is well known your God has told you He will give you the land from the Negev Desert in the south to the Lebanon mountains in the north, from the Euphrates River in the east to the Mediterranean Sea in the west. These are the lands of the Canaanites, the Hittites, the Amorites, the Perizzites, the Hivites, and the Jebusites. We do not fear your armies, but we do fear your God! And we realize our city stands between your people and the rest of the land."

The two men were no longer trying to conceal their identity, so I continued.

"The two of you have obviously been sent to spy on our city and its defenses. It was likely just as obvious to Chemosh when you encountered him at the gate. I believe your God has brought the three of us together because I can help you – and in turn, you can help me!"

"Why would you help us?" Iru asked.

"I have my reasons," I replied, "but, at this moment, they are not your concern."

Suddenly there was a loud pounding on the door, and a voice called out, "Rahab, open this door. I have a message for you from the king!"

I looked at the two men and said, "Very soon, I will need to trust you. But for right now, you must trust me. Follow me! Quickly!"

I hurriedly led them out onto the roof and told the men to hide amid the bundles of flax being stored there. Once I knew they were out of sight, I opened the door to receive Chemosh and the two guards accompanying him.

~

18

A PROMISE GIVEN

~

*C*hemosh was red in the face when I opened the door. "What took
you so long to open this door?" he demanded. "Could you not
hear it was me when I announced I was here on the king's business?"

"Chief Counselor, I always want to look my best when I am receiving
someone of your stature and importance," I replied. "Surely you can
understand that."

"Never mind all that," he said. *"Some Israelites have come here tonight to spy
out our land.* The king has sent me to arrest those men. Your neighbors said
they saw you with them. *Bring out the men who have come into* the inn."[1]

"Yes, the men were here earlier," I replied, *"but I didn't know where they were
from. They left the town at dusk, as the gates were about to close. I don't know
where they went. But if you hurry, you can probably catch up with them."*[2]

Chemosh stared at me, obviously trying to decide if I was telling the truth. After a few moments he turned to his guards and said, "Come! We have wasted enough time here! We must find them before the sun goes down!"

I waited for a while to see if they would return, then finally went back to the roof. I knew the spies had heard my exchange with Chemosh and were aware I turned him away. *"I know your God has given you this land,"* I said to them. *"We are all afraid of you. Everyone in the land is living in terror. No one has the courage to fight after hearing what your God has done. For the Lord your God is the supreme God of the heavens above and the earth below.*[(3)]

"Now swear to me by the Lord that you will be kind to me and my family since I have helped you. Give me some guarantee that when Jericho is conquered, you will let me live, along with my father and mother, my brothers and sisters, and all their families."[(4)]

Elah was the first to answer. *"We offer our own lives as a guarantee for your safety. If you don't betray us, we will keep our promise and be kind to you when the Lord gives us the land."*[(5)]

Since the inn is built into the town wall – providing a good escape route – I let them down by a rope through my bedroom window. *"Escape to the hill country,"* I told them. *"Hide there for three days from the men searching for you. Then, when they have returned, you can go on your way."*[(6)]

Before they left, Iru told me, *"We will be bound by the oath we have taken only if you follow these instructions. When we come into the land, you must leave this scarlet rope hanging from the window through which you let us down. And all your family members – your father, mother, brothers, and all your relatives – must be here inside the house. If they go out into the street and are killed, it will not be our fault. But if anyone lays a hand on people inside this house, we will accept the responsibility for their death. If you betray us, however, we are not bound by this oath in any way."*[(7)]

"*I accept your terms,*"[8] I replied. After the men climbed down the wall and scurried away, I pulled the rope back into my bedroom, leaving a portion hanging from the window. Next, I needed to tell my mother, my father, and Chusor about my conversation with the spies.

I arranged for the four of us to meet the next night in my bed chamber. They listened intently as I told them the promise I had been given. Like me, they knew the threat of the Israelites – and more specifically, their God – was imminent. But now their God, through these spies, had promised to keep us safe!

My parents and Chusor's reactions were similar to mine. First, we were all gratified to know that the king, his counselor, and his priest would finally have their day of reckoning. That day could not come too soon as far as we were concerned!

But, as we thought of their destruction, we also thought of the city that had always been our home, and our neighbors who lived here. We were saddened by the knowledge of what would befall them and discussed whether there was a way we could save them. But the reality was we could not. The promise had been specific to those who would be with me in the inn when the Israelites came.

In addition to the four of us, my two brothers, their wives and children, there were fourteen priestesses and twelve attendants. Half served in the temple, and the remainder in the inn. They were all my family – and they would be protected! Those who served at the inn would already be there when the time came, so they wouldn't be a problem. But we needed to devise a plan to have my mother and those from the temple come join us inside the inn at the right moment.

We knew the timing would be critical. They couldn't come to the inn too soon or Mawat and others would become suspicious. And it would need to be done in a way that did not draw attention to them. When the time came, they would each need to leave their temple garments behind and wear clothing that enabled them to blend in with everyone else.

Chusor spoke up. "We will need a distraction that turns the attention of Mawat and the others away from us. I will take responsibility for that."

"Just make sure you make it to the inn in time as well," I added. "The spies were very clear when they said that anyone in the street could not be protected."

"Then I will make sure I am not in the street!" he replied with a grin.

Chusor was actually more like a brother to me than my younger brothers. And though I trusted Elyon and Rimmon, I knew they wouldn't be able to keep anything I told them from their wives. We all agreed we could not risk their knowing about the plan for now. We would tell them when the time was right.

The next day, Chusor reported that Chemosh and his guards had returned to the city. The king had not been pleased to hear the spies had escaped!

∾

19

AN UNPREDICTABLE GOD

❧

Four days after the spies left Jericho, a warning spread quicky throughout the city. "The Israelites have moved their camp and are now settled on the eastern bank of the Jordan River!"

King Aleyin sent Chemosh with a cohort of soldiers to spy on the Israelites' movement from the western bank. Chemosh was to continually send back reports of his observations. One of Chusor's spies worked in the king's palace, so we received those reports almost as quickly as the king.

The Israelites were camped up and down the riverbank as far as the eye could see. Chemosh estimated their number at almost 2 million, including women and children. In one of Chemosh's first reports, he wrote, "The Israelites have chosen the absolute worst time of year to cross the Jordan. The river is at flood stage overflowing its banks. There is no way they can cross the river now. I expect they will have to wait for at least another month or two before they can even attempt it."

"Well, if that's the case, we still have time to gain the assistance of the other northern cities," Aleyin declared to his council. "Take this message to King Jabin of Hazor, King Jobab of Madon, King Adoni-zedek of Jerusalem, and all the other northern kings: 'The Israelites are approaching. We estimate their arrival at Jericho's gate in thirty days. Mobilize your warriors and come quickly to help us fight this enemy, so together we might destroy them before they endanger any of your cities.'"

The messengers were dispatched far and wide. But Aleyin and Chemosh had underestimated the power of the God of the Israelites! The Israelites remained encamped by the river for three days, which seemed to confirm Chemosh's expectation. However, on the fourth day, there was movement in the camp. Chemosh could not believe his eyes!

This was his report to Aleyin: "Four men dressed like priests are carrying a large golden box between them. It appears to be an ark of some kind that they must use in the worship of their God. They walked to the edge of the riverbank with the golden box and then took a few steps into the river. Suddenly the water stopped flowing from somewhere upriver! The remaining waters continued their journey on down to the sea.

"The priests then proceeded to walk on what now was a dry riverbed. They stopped in the center of the two riverbanks and are allowing the remaining people to walk across to the other side. The Israelites will be on our western shore before nightfall! I have never witnessed anything like this. These people cannot be doing this. It is an act of their God!"

Later that day, Chemosh sent a second message. "The Israelites, except for the four priests, have now completed their journey to the western shore. Twelve men gathered twenty-four stones from the place the priests were standing in the center of the riverbed. They have built two structures, each with twelve of the stones. One is in the riverbed where the priests were standing, and the other is on the western shore. I do not know any possible military purpose for these structures. They must be memorials to what their God has done.

"But the most amazing thing is that once those structures were built, the priests completed their journey across the dry riverbed. My king, once they reached the shore, the Jordan River flooded its banks as before! It was if the waters had never stopped. And now, our enemies are less than a day's journey from our gates!"

Fear set in as that message circulated from household to household. The people of Jericho began to lose hope and cried out to their gods. Aleyin knew no other armies would be coming to help them. He called out to Baal and Asherah to protect the city of Jericho behind its great walls.

The Israelites set up camp for the night on the western shore as Chemosh and his soldiers continued to watch from a short distance away. They were close enough to hear the Israelite leader, whose name I later learned was Joshua, when he declared, "Make for yourselves knives of flint. It is time for us to be a circumcised people again. All the men and boys born since our exodus from Egypt are now to be circumcised in obedience to the covenant our patriarch Abraham made with our Lord God."

The next message Chemosh sent to Aleyin was more hopeful. "My king, you will not believe what is happening now! The flesh of the foreskin of every man and boy under forty years of age has been cut off. The men are lying down on their mats; they are in too much pain to even think about fighting. These are a very strange people! They have taken forty years to arrive at our gates – and now they do this? I do not know what to tell you, my king. As soon as I think I know what they are about to do, they do something completely unexpected. I will continue to keep you informed."

Three days passed while the Israelite men healed from their circumcisions. Then the following day, Chemosh heard Joshua announce, "This evening we will celebrate Passover. It marks the day of our exodus from Egypt forty years ago. Prepare unleavened bread, harvest grain from the land, and roast it. Tonight, we will eat the Passover supper in remembrance of what our God has done for us."

Chemosh's message to Aleyin that night simply read; "Tonight they are eating a celebratory meal. I no longer have any idea what the next day will bring!"

The gates of Jericho remained tightly shut; no one was allowed to go in or out. The temple and inn were now filled with anxious men who were no longer able to work outside the walls. They were coming to spend time with the priestesses and call out to Asherah to save them.

But I knew Asherah would never hear their cry. She had never been able to hear them. But the Lord God of the Israelites was very capable of doing whatever He intended ... and by His grace, He had promised to save me and my family. And that day would soon be upon us!

~

20

A STRANGE WAY TO DEFEAT A CITY

～

A watchman on top of the city wall called out, "The Israelites are here!" His cry was soon followed by the sounds of rams' horns being blown. It had been thirteen days since the two spies had given me their promise. Was today the day? Did Chusor need to get the temple servants to the inn immediately?

Though fear seized the heart of most everyone in the city, it was also mixed with curiosity. Everyone had heard of the Israelites and their God – but now we could see them in person. People began to peek out their windows or climb on top of the walls to get a glimpse. And the approaching processional was quite a sight!

As I watched from the inn, I saw a contingent of armed guards walking at the very front. Right behind them were seven priests blowing rams' horns. Following them were four priests carrying the golden box we had all heard about. I now know the box is called the Ark of the Covenant containing the tablets God gave to Moses. Behind the Ark was another contingent of armed guards.

The balance of the Israelite army, approximately 600,000 strong, followed. When they arrived at the city, they did not proceed to the gates; rather, they kept marching. They marched completely around the city and, to my surprise, they didn't make a sound, other than that of the seven rams' horns. Each man walked in silence. They were not doing anything one would expect an attacking army to do to intimidate their victims.

I could see the quizzical expressions of the other Jerichoites staring out their windows, as if to say, "What are these men doing?" If our people hadn't been so fearful, it would have been comical. It was a surreal moment.

I wondered if the army would attack our gates once they finished walking around the city walls. Apparently, Aleyin and Chemosh had the same thought because they ordered their soldiers to prepare for battle. But after the Israelites completed one circuit around the city, they marched back to their camp.

Though I have no military experience, even I thought it was an unusual battle strategy. Did they change their minds? Did they decide our walls were too impenetrable? Had our forebearers been right and had the hundred years of labor to build the walls paid off? Were we truly an unconquerable city?

My heart sank. Was the promise the Israelite spies had given me all for nothing? Were they not going to conquer our city? Was their God unable to defeat our walls? Were all of my hopes that the Israelites would bring about the downfall of my enemies unmerited? What was happening?

Overwhelming relief permeated the rest of the city. Townspeople concluded that the Israelites had chosen to just walk away. No one could believe their eyes.

Having seen the size of their army, Aleyin knew it would be foolish to engage the Israelites outside the city; our army was massively outnumbered. So, an attack wasn't an option. He sent Chemosh and a cohort back out to spy on the Israelites so he could try and gain an advantage.

Chemosh soon reported back. "The Israelites have returned to their encampment and are settling in for the remainder of the day. I do not see any activity to suggest they are leaving or reformulating a battle plan. My king, I do not understand this people – or their God!"

The temple and inn were still filled with men seeking time with the priestesses, but they seemed to be less anxious. It was as if the entire city had taken a great sigh of relief and was now waiting to see what was next.

The next morning, the Israelites arrived at the city walls at the same time in the same formation as before. And again, they silently marched around the city before proceeding back to their encampment.

My mother, father, Chusor, and I met that evening to discuss what was happening.

"Mawat has been saying the God of the Israelites is afraid of our god Baal," Chusor told us. "He said Baal will protect us and somehow bring the Israelites to utter defeat by our hands when the other Canaanite armies come to assist us. Mawat is pleased the coffers at the temple are increasing. He even joked about sending the Israelites a message to thank them for creating such a stir."

"I would venture that the God of the Israelites is not one to be mocked," I responded. "And I would further predict that Mawat will soon regret his words. But then again, he has much for which he should regret."

"Yes, but what about the Israelites?" my father asked. "Are they truly able to conquer this city? Is their promise to be believed?"

"I do not know what is happening," I replied, "but I do believe we can trust the God of the Israelites. Four days ago, Chemosh thought they wouldn't be able to cross the river for a month or two, and their God made a way. Do not be deceived by the foolish utterings of people like Mawat. The Israelites' God will lead them to conquer this city!"

We parted ways and agreed to trust the promise we had been given. However, for the next four days, the same thing occurred. By the fourth day, our people were no longer standing by quietly; their fear was gone. Now they stood on the walls and at their windows mocking the Israelites and their God. Some were even daring the Israelites to attack us.

The temple and the inn were almost empty while the Israelites marched around the city. Our patrons preferred to hurl insults and scorn them. On the seventh day, Mawat and Chemosh joined Aleyin on top of the wall to taunt and ridicule the Israelites. I sent word to Chusor to bring the temple priestesses and attendants to the inn. I knew in my heart this was going to be the moment!

~

21

THE WALLS CRUMBLED

~

*T*his time the Israelites did not march back to their encampment after they walked around the city walls. Instead, they continued around the perimeter a second time . . . then a third . . . and a fourth. By then, the Jerichoites' jeering was starting to die down. They knew something was about to happen.

In the meantime, Chusor arrived at the inn with the other attendants and priestesses. I had just told my brothers about the promise I had been given by the spies. Gratefully, they had not questioned me, and they and their families joined us in the safety of the inn.

Chusor told me he was going to remain just outside the inn so he could keep an eye on Aleyin, Chemosh, and Mawat from a distance. None of us trusted them and we had all come to expect the unexpected from them. So, until the Israelites made their move, we needed to know what those three men were doing. I reminded Chusor to stay close. "Remember, when the Israelites attack, you need to be inside the inn!"

As the army marched around the walls a sixth time, Chusor saw Mawat leave the wall and head toward the temple. Chusor knew if Mawat got to the temple and saw everyone was missing, he would sound an alarm. We couldn't risk the possibility of guards being dispatched to the inn to remove us. Chusor called out to me that he was going to the temple to stop Mawat.

After the Israelites completed their seventh march around the city, I became concerned because Chusor had not returned. I considered running to the temple to get him. But before I could act, the sound from the rams' horns changed into a long, eerie blast. It was immediately followed by the mountainous shouts of all 600,000 men, as if they spoke with one voice.

Suddenly the walls of the city collapsed, crumbling into fine debris. Structures throughout the city began to break apart. People on top of the walls fell to their death. The collapsing rock and stone fell on those on the ground. In a matter of moments, the entire city and all its inhabitants had been destroyed – except those of us inside the inn.

We looked at one another in disbelief. The only portion of the city wall left standing was the one to which our inn was attached. The only building remaining was the inn. It was as if the hand of God had encapsulated and protected us from the destruction all around.

People often ask me at what point I became a follower of the Lord God Jehovah. I tell them, without question, it was the moment I realized He had placed His hand of protection around us. And that is not only true for me; it is true of all of us He sheltered in the inn. Our lives changed that day in more ways than I could ever adequately describe.

Within moments, I looked around to find Chusor. Had he made it back?

The Israelites were now overrunning the city. Everything outside the inn was in chaos. Iru and Elah arrived at my door in just a matter of minutes.

As soon as they saw me, Iru said, "Our God has kept His promise and shielded you all from harm. Now, you must come with us. This place is no longer safe. We will take you to our encampment."

"But I must find Chusor!" I cried out. "He was not inside the inn when the walls collapsed."

Iru looked at me sternly. "I told you we could not guarantee the safety of anyone who was not inside the inn."

"I know, but I must find him. He risked his life to protect us from being discovered and taken out of the inn. You take the others to your camp, and I will come join you after I find Chusor."

Iru hesitated, then said, "Elah will take your family to safety in our camp, and I will go with you to find Chusor."

Though Iru and I passed through rubble on our way to the temple, I wasn't prepared for what I saw. Our beautiful temple was now a pile of rock and stone. The ornate furnishings were demolished beyond recognition.

The golden statue of Asherah lay on the ground with her head, arms, and legs severed from her body. Her beautifully sculpted face was now twisted into a sinister expression. As I stared at her broken form, I realized this was what Asherah had always been. She wasn't the beautiful goddess we had spent our lives worshiping; rather, she was a piece of metal formed into the image we desired her to be. She was nothing more than what I now saw lying at my feet.

Suddenly a shimmer of reflected sunlight caught my attention. I turned toward a pile of rubble in the middle of what had once been the great hall. As I drew closer, I noticed a man's arm protruding from debris that completely covered the rest of his body. But I immediately recognized the ornate and jeweled sleeve of the priestly robe. It was Mawat.

I felt no sadness for this man's death. He had caused more pain and suffering to more people during his lifetime than anyone I knew. Now, he had literally fallen under the judgment of a holy God.

I continued to scan the area for any sign of Chusor. It was then I saw a hand extending out of the rocks near Mawat. I instinctively began to remove the rubble. This man's sleeve was a simple garment, not a priestly robe. Iru reached down and helped me uncover the body – I knew right away it was Chusor. Tears began to fall long before I was able to see his face.

Based on the position of the two bodies, it was obvious Chusor had been restraining Mawat. Chusor had prevented him from doing anything that might cause harm to those of us in the inn. My heart was broken for my lifelong friend who had sacrificed his life to save ours. I didn't even try to hold back the flood of tears.

~

22

A NEW TRIBE

~

"*R*ahab, we must go," Iru said firmly but with gentleness. "My people will be preparing to burn the city. We must leave now."

His words, at least for the moment, pulled me back from the depths of my sorrow. "Yes, let's go. I must see about the others."

As we made our way out of the city, we came upon an older man who was obviously the Israelite leader. He was commanding his men that only silver, gold, bronze, and iron were to be kept for the treasury of the Lord's house. Nothing else was to be taken; it was all to be burned.

Iru introduced me to the man whose name was Joshua. "Thank you for protecting Iru and Elah when they came to your city. I know you did so at great personal risk. We invite you and your people to come live among us as neighbors and not as enemies. You have done us a great service."

"And you have done us an even greater service," I responded. "You have introduced us to your God – the one, true God – the One whom we now follow. We look forward to learning more about Him from your people."

As Iru and I continued on to their camp, I heard Joshua declare:

> *"May the curse of the Lord fall on anyone*
> *who tries to rebuild the town of Jericho.*
> *At the cost of his firstborn son,*
> *he will lay its foundation.*
> *At the cost of his youngest son,*
> *he will set up its gates."*[1]

As we walked a little farther, we saw a man rallying the warriors around him. He appeared to be the same age as Joshua, but he was clearly able to keep pace with the much younger men who surrounded him. "Rahab, this is my father, Caleb," Iru said as he introduced us.

"I will forever be in your debt, Rahab," Caleb said, "for protecting my sons. They have told me about the courage you demonstrated and the risks you took on their behalf. My sons and I are of the tribe of Judah. We would be honored if you and your household would come and live in our midst."

"You honor us with your invitation, and we would be most pleased to do so," I replied. "Jehovah God led me to meet your sons and through them He has protected us. So we will always be indebted to your family as well."

"Then you and your household must join my family for our evening meal tonight," Caleb continued. "It will provide an opportunity for our families to get to know one another."

"We will be honored," I answered with gratitude for his welcoming hospitality.

Iru and I continued our journey to the encampment. I was soon reunited with my family who were staring at these new and different people who surrounded them. We were all just beginning the process of learning the Israelites' ways and beliefs. We were no longer Jerichoites, but it would be a while before we were truly seen as Israelites. In the meantime, we needed to learn how to fit in.

We no longer considered ourselves priestesses or attendants; we were now simply women and men. We knew the one we had worshiped was a false god, and we no longer wanted to continue any practice that would remind us of her. Our temple garments had been destroyed when Jericho burned to the ground. And all of us women disposed of the pastes and polishes we had been taught to use to adorn our faces in order to beguile men.

Perhaps, most importantly, we no longer carried out a trade that had always euphemistically been referred to as worship. Those of us who survived needed to learn practical skills that would help us thrive in our new lives.

Our transition to becoming Israelites was not without its challenges. It was a process! But our new neighbors helped us adapt. And they graciously provided us with tents, clothing, and food when we first arrived. Most everyone did all they could to make us feel welcome.

The flurry of activity surrounding our arrival provided temporary relief from our grief. That first evening, we enjoyed a meal with Caleb, Iru, Elah, and their families. I was surprised there was not a boisterous celebration among a people who had just experienced such an overwhelming victory.

"Our people know the victory today belongs to the Lord," Caleb told me. "It had nothing to do with our ability or our effort. He alone destroyed the walls of your city. He alone is worthy of praise and worship. We mourn the lives lost today. But we know those lives were lost because your people rejected the one true God. By your own admission that day to my sons, your people knew our God. Your people feared Him but did not accept Him. Rather, the people of Jericho turned to their own gods.

"And the Lord God Jehovah is a jealous God. He has told us we are to have no other gods before Him. And He is a just God. He has said He will not leave unpunished the sins of those who reject Him. We were all witnesses to His justness and His punishment today. But you and your family were also witnesses to His love, His faithfulness, and His protection as He held you in His hand.

"So, we do not celebrate victory tonight; rather, we celebrate His faithfulness. His faithfulness to the promise He gave our ancestors many years ago, to bring us into this land. And His faithfulness to you to protect you as He promised."

I looked around the circle at my friends and family as they listened to Caleb's words. No one needed any convincing that his words were truth, or that His God – the Lord God Jehovah – was the one true God, worthy of our love, our trust, and our worship. And by His grace, He had chosen to save us and rescue us from the lives we had been living apart from Him.

∾

23

A NEW LIFE

~

*A*s the months passed, we integrated into life with the Israelites. We were constantly on the move. Jehovah God led us throughout Canaan as one city after another fell. The men in my family fought side by side with the Israelite warriors. It wasn't long before we felt more like Israelites than Canaanites. Our men even chose to become circumcised to enter into the covenant with Jehovah God.

Though the Canaanite kings did eventually band together in an attempt to stave off the Israelites' attacks, every effort was met with the same result – defeat! There was only one time we saw the Israelite army defeated. Ironically, it was against the smallest of cities – Ai.

The city should have fallen with minimal effort. But as it turned out, an Israelite named Achan, who also was of the tribe of Judah, had taken some of the possessions from Jericho – silver and gold meant for the Lord's treasury, and a robe that should have been burned. Because of his disobedience, God demonstrated His wrath and caused the Israelites to be defeated. Only once Achan's sin was revealed were the Israelites able to defeat Ai.

It was a reminder that God does not look the other way when we disobey Him. He calls us to walk righteously before Him according to His ways. It was a hard lesson that day – but in many ways, it is a lesson we are all still learning every day.

The women of my family have learned how to maintain a proper Israelite household. It required us to learn different ways of preparing our food, as well as selecting which foods we eat and which we do not. Israelite standards of cleanliness are much greater than anything we practiced in Jericho, even though we spent much of our time living in the open air. I found that I was not only accepting of the differences, I grew to embrace them.

The adjustment I enjoyed most, though, was learning how to worship Jehovah God with my whole heart, mind, and soul. I have much for which to thank and praise Him. He set me free and gave me a new life. He protected me – even before I realized it.

Then one day, I noticed a change in my attitude. Jehovah God had removed the anger and bitterness from my heart. Though Aleyin, Chemosh, and Mawat had died in Jericho, I had carried hatred for them long after their deaths. But Jehovah God had made me into a new person with a new outlook and a new way of life.

I saw a similar change in my parents. They, too, set aside the holdovers from their old way of life and embraced Jehovah God and their new life. It was most obvious in the way they now treated and loved each other. I had never questioned their affection for one another, but now the two truly had become one. I only regretted that my grandparents, Llisha and Ashima, never had the opportunity to experience this new life.

It was a delight to watch changes occur in the lives of my brothers and their families, as well as my other "brothers and sisters." In many ways, we had all been one large family at the temple and the inn, and now we really were one. The former priestesses and attendants viewed Kothar and

Liluri as their father and mother, and my parents considered them as their children. Over time, they saw their "sons" and "daughters" marry – a few to one another – but mostly, to Israelite men and women.

Soon after we arrived in the Israelite camp, I met a man by the name of Salmon. He also belonged to the tribe of Judah. His father, Nahshon, was one of the leaders of the tribe like Caleb. But he died while the Israelites were still camped on the east side of the Jordan River. Salmon was his eldest son and a very kind and gentle man.

He became one of the six men I have truly loved in my life. The first was brave and gentle Llisha, my grandfather, who always watched out for me. The second is Kothar, the only real father I have ever known. The third was Chusor, my friend since childhood, who literally gave up his life so I and others could live.

The fourth is Caleb. He has become my spiritual father and counselor. It is through his teaching, as we sit around the fire each night, that I have learned about Jehovah God. Sometimes when I look at Caleb, I feel as if I am looking into the face of God.

The fifth is Salmon. By the grace and providence of Jehovah God, we became husband and wife two years after the walls of Jericho fell. He is so much more than I could have ever hoped for in a husband. I had never envisioned that I would marry. Other than my father and grandfather, I had always found it difficult to trust men; they could too easily betray you. But God used Salmon to teach me that is not the case. My husband taught me how to love openly, freely, and completely. It is a joy I never anticipated.

The sixth man is one I loved from the instant I felt him move in my womb – my son, Boaz. Two years after Salmon and I married, God blessed us with our precious boy. He is now six years of age, and the excellent qualities of the other five men are already noticeable in him.

There is no question Jehovah God has redeemed me. He set me free from the walled prison in which I lived. Yes, in some ways it was a prison made for me by others – but even more so, it was the prison of my own sin. There was nothing about me to merit His redemption – and yet, He looked upon me and had mercy.

I have asked God to help me be an instrument of His redemption to another. Perhaps, it will be someone like me – one who is without hope apart from His sovereign grace. If not in my lifetime, perhaps that redemption will come about through my son. Who knows what Jehovah God might do through Boaz to redeem such a one!

∾

PLEASE HELP ME BY LEAVING A REVIEW!

i would be very grateful if you would leave a review of this book. Your feedback will be helpful to me in my future writing endeavors and will also assist others as they consider picking up a copy of the book.

To leave a review:

Go to: amazon.com/dp/1956866140

Or scan this QR code using your camera on your smartphone:

Thanks for your help!

~

YOU WILL WANT TO READ ALL OF THE BOOKS IN "THE CALLED" SERIES

Stories of these ordinary men and women called by God to be used in extraordinary ways.

A Carpenter Called Joseph (Book 1)

A Prophet Called Isaiah (Book 2)

A Teacher Called Nicodemus (Book 3)

A Judge Called Deborah (Book 4)

A Merchant Called Lydia (Book 5)

A Friend Called Enoch (Book 6)

A Fisherman Called Simon (Book 7)

A Heroine Called Rahab (Book 8)

A Witness Called Mary (Book 9) releasing March 24

A Cupbearer Called Nehemiah (Book 10) releasing June 16

IF YOU ENJOYED THIS STORY ABOUT RAHAB ...

... you will want to read this novel about the Israelite spy Caleb

Caleb was one of God's chosen people — a people to whom He had given a promise. Caleb never forgot that promise — as a slave in Egypt, a spy in the Promised Land, a wanderer in the wilderness, or a conqueror in the hill country.

Walk with him and see the promise of Jehovah God unfold through his eyes, and **experience a story of God's faithfulness – to a spy who trusted Him – and to each one of us who will do the same.**

AVAILABLE IN PAPERBACK, LARGE PRINT, AND FOR KINDLE (OR YOUR KINDLE APP) ON AMAZON.

To order your copy:

Go to: amazon.com/dp/1734193018

Or scan this QR code using your camera on your smartphone:

~

THROUGH THE EYES

... the complete *"THROUGH THE EYES"* SERIES

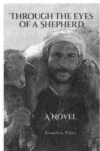  

Experience the truths of Scripture as these stories unfold through the lives and eyes of a shepherd, a spy and a prisoner. Rooted in biblical truth, these fictional novels will enable you to draw beside the storytellers as they worship the Baby in the manger, the Son who took up the cross, the Savior who conquered the grave, the Deliverer who parted the sea and the Eternal God who has always had a mission.

Through the Eyes of a Shepherd (Book 1)

Through the Eyes of a Spy (Book 2)

Through the Eyes of a Prisoner (Book 3)

AVAILABLE IN PAPERBACK, LARGE PRINT, AND FOR KINDLE ON AMAZON.

Scan this QR code using your camera on your smartphone to see the entire series on Amazon:

THE EYEWITNESSES COLLECTION

... you will also want to read "The Eyewitnesses" Collection

The first four books in these collections of short stories chronicle the first person eyewitness accounts of eighty-five men, women and children and their unique relationships with Jesus.

Little Did We Know – the advent of Jesus (Book 1)

Not Too Little To Know – the advent – ages 8 thru adult (Book 2)

The One Who Stood Before Us – the ministry and passion of Jesus (Book 3)

The Little Ones Who Came – the ministry and passion – ages 8 thru adult (Book 4)

The Patriarchs — eyewitnesses from the beginning — Adam through Moses tell their stories (Book 5) — releasing in 2023

AVAILABLE IN PAPERBACK, LARGE PRINT, AND FOR KINDLE ON AMAZON.

Scan this QR code using your camera on your smartphone to see the entire collection on Amazon:

LESSONS LEARNED IN THE WILDERNESS

The Lessons Learned In The Wilderness series

A non-fiction series of devotional studies

There are lessons that can only be learned in the wilderness experiences of our lives. As we see throughout the Bible, God is right there leading us each and every step of the way, if we will follow Him. Wherever we are, whatever we are experiencing, He will use it to enable us to experience His Person, witness His power and join Him in His mission.

The Journey Begins (Exodus) – Book 1

The Wandering Years (Numbers and Deuteronomy) – Book 2

Possessing The Promise (Joshua and Judges) – Book 3

Walking With The Master (The Gospels leading up to Palm Sunday) – Book 4

Taking Up The Cross (The Gospels – the passion through ascension) – Book 5

Until He Returns (The Book of Acts) – Book 6

The complete series is also available in two e-book boxsets or two single soft-cover print volumes.

AVAILABLE IN PAPERBACK AND FOR KINDLE ON AMAZON.

Scan this QR code using your camera on your smartphone to see the entire series on Amazon:

——————

For more information, go to:

wildernesslessons.com or kenwinter.org

ALSO AVAILABLE AS AN AUDIOBOOK

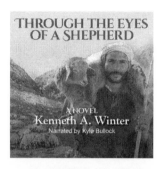

For more information on how you can order your audiobook, go to kenwinter.org/audiobooks

SCRIPTURE BIBLIOGRAPHY

∼

The basis for the story line of this book is taken from the Book of Joshua.

Certain fictional events or depictions of those events have been added.

Some of the dialogue in this story are direct quotations from Scripture. Here are the specific references for those quotations:

Preface

[1] Hebrews 11:31

[2] Exodus 34:7

Chapter 2

[1] Genesis 9:25

Chapter 18

[1] Joshua 2:2-3

[2] Joshua 2:4-5

(3) Joshua 2:9,11

(4) Joshua 2:12-13

(5) Joshua 2:14

(6) Joshua 2:16

(7) Joshua 2:17-20

(8) Joshua 2:21

Chapter 22

(1) Joshua 6:26

∾

LISTING OF CHARACTERS
(ALPHABETICAL ORDER)

~

Many of the characters in this book are individuals pulled directly from the pages of Scripture. i have not changed any details about a number of those individuals except the addition of their interactions with the fictional characters. They are noted below as "UN" (unchanged).

In other instances, fictional details have been added to real people to provide backgrounds about their lives where Scripture is silent. The intent is that you understand these were real people, whose lives were full of all of the many details that fill our own lives. They are noted as "FB" (fictional background).

In some instances, we are never told the names of certain individuals in the Bible. In those instances, where i have given them a name as well as a fictional background, they are noted as "FN" (fictional name).

Lastly, a number of the characters are purely fictional, added to convey the fictional elements of these stories. They are noted as "FC" (fictional character).

Abraham – patriarch of the Israelites (UN)

Achan – a member of the tribe of Judah who disobeyed God and removed treasures from Jericho (UN)

Adoni-zedek – king of Jerusalem (UN)

Ahmose I – king of Egypt 1569-1544 (UN)

Aleyin – son of Arsu, third king of Jericho (1479-1439), father of Lotan, walls finished under his reign (17th gen after Noah) (FN)

Amenhotep – king of Egypt 1544-1520 (UN)

Arsu – son of Attar, second king of Jericho (1518-1479), father of Aleyin, birth father of Liluri and Rahab (16th gen after Noah) (FC)

Ashima – daughter of Kusor & Pidraya, priestess to King Arsu, mother of Liluri, grandmother of Rahab (FC)

Asherah – pagan goddess of the Canaanites, consort of Baal (UN)

Attar – son of Hadad, first king of Jericho (1547-1518), father of Arsu (15th gen after Noah) (FC)

Baal – pagan deity of the Canaanites (UN)

Boaz – son of Salmon & Rahab, kinsman redeemer of Ruth (UN)

Caleb – tribal leader of Judah, father of Iru & Elah (FB)

Canaan – son of Ham (born after flood) (2nd gen after Noah) (UN)

Chemosh – chief counselor & general to King Aleyin (FC)

Chusor – son of Talaya, lifelong friend of Rahab (FC)

Elah – younger son of Caleb, Israelite spy sent to Jericho (FB)

Elyon – eldest son of Kothar & Liluri, brother of Rahab (FC)

Hadad – eldest son of Malakbel, a leader of Jericho, father of Attar, co-architect of Jericho walls (14th gen after Noah) (FC)

Ham – second son of Noah (UN)

Iru – eldest son of Caleb, Israelite spy sent to Jericho (FB)

Ishtar – chief priestess (1527-1479) (FC)

Jabin – king of Hazor (UN)

Japheth – third son of Noah (UN)

Jobab – king of Madon (UN)

Joshua – leader of the Israelites (UN)

Kirta – son of Shachar, father of Llisha, executed by his cousin, King Attar (15th gen after Noah) (FC)

Kothar – chief attendant of inn (1496-1439), childhood friend and husband of Liluri, parental father to Rahab, Elyon & Rimmon (FN)

Kusor – husband of Pidraya, father of Ashima, great-grandfather of Rahab (FC)

Liluri – chief priestess (1479-1439), illegitimate daughter of King Arsu, daughter of Ashima, wife of Kothar, mother of Rahab, Elyon & Rimmon (FN)

Llisha – son of Kirta, eunuch, companion of Ashima, surrogate grandfather of Rahab (16th gen after Noah) (FC)

Lot – nephew of Abraham (UN)

Lotan – eldest son of Aleyin, prince of Jericho (18th gen after Noah) (FC)

Malakbel – father of Hadad & Shachar (13th gen after Noah) (FC)

Mawat – chief priest installed by King Aleyin (FC)

Nahshon – leader of the tribe of Judah, father of Salmon (UN)

Noah – son of Lamech (UN)

Og – an Amorite king of Bashan (UN)

Pidraya – wife of Kusor, mother of Ashima, great-grandmother of Rahab (FC)

Rahab – daughter of Liluri & Kothar (illegitimate daughter of King Arsu), priestess to Prince Lotan, chief priestess over the inn, wife of Salmon, mother of Boaz (17th gen after Noah) (FB)

Resheph – pagan lord of the netherworld (UN)

Rimmon – younger son of Kothar & Liluri, brother of Rahab (FC)

Salmon – son of Nahshon, husband of Rahab, father of Boaz (FB)

Shachar – second son of Malakbel, co-architect of Jericho walls, great-great-grandfather of Rahab (14th gen after Noah) (FC)

Shahar – high counselor to King Arsu (FC)

Shem – eldest son of Noah (UN)

Sihon – an Amorite king of Heshbon (UN)

Talaya – priestess to King Aleyin, mother of Chusor (FC)

Thutmose I – king of Egypt 1520-1492 (UN)

Thutmose II (Amenemhat) – king of Egypt 1492-1479, died in the Red Sea (FB)

Thutmose III – king of Egypt 1479-1425 (UN)

Unnamed children of Elyon – nieces & nephews of Rahab (FC)

Unnamed children of Rimmon – nieces & nephews of Rahab (FC)

Unnamed kings of the northern kingdoms of Canaan (UN)

Unnamed servant of Mawat (FC)

Unnamed wife of Elyon (FC)

Unnamed wife of Rimmon (FC)

∼

ACKNOWLEDGMENTS

I do not cease to give thanks for you ….
Ephesians 1:16 (ESV)

… my partner and heroine in all things, LaVonne,
for choosing to trust God as we walk with Him in this faith adventure;

… my family,
for your continuing love, support and encouragement;

… Sheryl,
i'll keep writing as long as you keep editing;

… Scott,
for your heart for the mission of God;

… a precious group of advance readers,
who encourage and challenge me in the journey;

… and most importantly,
the One who goes before me in all things
– **my Lord and Savior Jesus Christ!**

∾

ABOUT THE AUTHOR

Ken Winter is a follower of Jesus, an extremely blessed husband, and a proud father and grandfather – all by the grace of God. His journey with Jesus has led him to serve on the pastoral staffs of two local churches – one in West Palm Beach, Florida and the other in Richmond, Virginia – and as the vice president of mobilization of the IMB, an international missions organization.

Today, Ken continues in that journey as a full-time author, teacher and speaker. You can read his weekly blog posts at kenwinter.blog and listen to his weekly podcast at kenwinter.org/podcast.

And we proclaim Him, admonishing every man and teaching every man with all wisdom, that we may present every man complete in Christ. And for this purpose also I labor, striving according to His power, which mightily works within me.
(Colossians 1:28-29 NASB)

PLEASE JOIN MY READERS' GROUP

Please join my Readers' Group in order to receive updates and information about future releases, etc.

Also, i will send you a free copy of *The Journey Begins* e-book — the first book in the *Lessons Learned In The Wilderness* series. It is yours to keep or share with a friend or family member that you think might benefit from it.

It's completely free to sign up. i value your privacy and will not spam you. Also, you can unsubscribe at any time.

Go to kenwinter.org to subscribe.

Or scan this QR code using your camera on your smartphone:

~

Made in the USA
Monee, IL
26 May 2023